"An Affair In The Workplace Is Never A Smart Move," Spencer Said.

"People are asking for problems when they allow that sort of thing to happen."

He paused to see if Jade was listening.

"Once you start making eyes at someone, it's only a matter of time before things get out of hand and you're getting caught between the filing cabinets. Then it's—"

"But we *don't* work together." She turned around to face him. "And what's more, you're not *my* type. So I most certainly could not imagine us making love on top of a desk."

"Who said anything about making love on top of a desk?"

"You just did. You said—" The unfinished sentence hung in the air, and her flushed face deepened to scarlet.

Spencer didn't bother correcting her. They both knew she'd realized her mistake and was paying dearly for it. And besides that, he was too busy watching her perfectly pouty lips parting in shock.

Or was it something else? That one-of-a-kind something that both of them had been fighting…

Dear Reader,

There's something for everyone this month! Brides, babies and cowboys…but also humor, sensuality…and delicious love stories (some without a baby in sight!).

There's nothing as wonderful as a new book from Barbara Boswell, and this month we have a MAN OF THE MONTH written by this talented author. *Who's the Boss?* is a very sexy, delightfully funny love story. As always, Barbara not only creates a masterful hero and smart-as-a-whip heroine, she also makes her secondary characters come alive!

When a pregnant woman gets stuck in a traffic jam she does the only thing she can do—talks a handsome hunk into giving her a ride to the hospital on his motorcycle in Leanne Banks's latest, *The Troublemaker Bride*.

Have you ever wanted to marry a millionaire? Well, heroine Irish Ellison plans on finding a man with money in *One Ticket to Texas* by Jan Hudson. A single mom-to-be gets a new life in Paula Detmer Riggs's emotional and heartwarming *Daddy by Accident*. And a woman with a "bad reputation" finds unexpected romance in Barbara McMahon's *Boss Lady and the Hired Hand*.

Going to your high-school reunion is bad enough. But what if you were voted "Most likely to succeed"…but your success at love has been fleeting? Well, that's just what happens in Susan Connell's *How To Succeed at Love*.

So read…and enjoy!

Lucia Macro

Lucia Macro
Senior Editor

Please address questions and book requests to:
Silhouette Reader Service
U.S.: 3010 Walden Ave., P.O. Box 1325, Buffalo, NY 14269
Canadian: P.O. Box 609, Fort Erie, Ont. L2A 5X3

SUSAN CONNELL
HOW TO SUCCEED AT LOVE

SILHOUETTE *Desire*®

Published by Silhouette Books

America's Publisher of Contemporary Romance

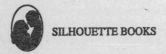

SILHOUETTE BOOKS

ISBN 0-373-76074-4

HOW TO SUCCEED AT LOVE

Copyright © 1997 by Susan Connell

Books by Susan Connell

Silhouette Desire

†*Reese: The Untamed* #981
*	*Rebel's Spirit* #1044
*	*How To Succeed at Love* #1074

†Sons and Lovers
*The Girls Most Likely To...

SUSAN CONNELL

has a love of traveling that has taken her all over the
world—Greece, Spain, Portugal, Central and South
America, to name just a few places. While working for
the foreign service she met a U.S. Navy pilot, and eight
days later they were engaged. Twenty-one years and several moves later, Susan, her husband, Jim, and daughter,
Catherine, call the New Jersey shore home. When she's
not writing, her part-time job at a local bookstore,
Mediterranean cooking and traveling with her family are
some of her favorite activities. Susan has been honored
by New Jersey Romance Writers with their coveted
Golden Leaf Award. She loves hearing from her readers.

Jim Connell, Cathy Connell,
Candace Cowdrick and Roger Cohen
For your expertise, sense of
humor and unfailing support.

One

"**S**moochie?"

The baritone voice came from inches away, but as far as Jade Macleod was concerned, the sound could have been from Mars.

Was she losing her mind? Did someone just offer her a kiss? Or was this an auditory hallucination brought on by stress? Pressing her hand against the front of her gray, pin-striped business suit, she cautiously turned away from the train window to the man sitting beside her.

"I beg your pardon?"

"Smoochie?" he repeated, giving her a lopsided grin that made her forget to breathe. He lowered his thick, dark lashes toward the foil-wrapped chocolate in his hand then back to her. "You look as if you could use one."

With everything she had to think about, it should have been easy to turn away. But the inviting combination of a handsome hunk with a funny line and her favorite brand of chocolate was making her mouth water. She swallowed; she'd never felt such deprivation in all of her twenty-eight years. And that trust-me twinkle in his big blue eyes wasn't helping. Then again, *this was not a big decision.*

Jade slowly brushed her fingers through her bangs. As she resettled the curvy, red locks on her forehead, her stare shifted to his trim, broad-shouldered body. He moved his hand closer to hers, causing her gaze to skim down to the candy before settling on his hand. The kind of hand that inspired thoughts of strength, reliability and gentle touches in the moonlight.

His corded wrists and muscled forearms were covered in a light sprinkling of hair all the way to where the pushed-up sleeves of his sweater bunched at his elbows. Her gaze drifted to his lap. His well-worn jeans defined every muscle, every angle and everything else within the masculine sprawl of his long legs. The same long legs that had been casually bumping against hers in time with the rhythmic swaying of the train car. Blinking, she moved her leg away from his and looked up.

His knowing and riveting stare was there to meet hers. Her lips parted in astonishment. What was she doing staring at his body like that? A plague of problems had descended on both her professional world and her personal world. She had major decisions to make. The last thing she should be thinking about was taking candy from a stranger.

"No, thank you."

"Spence. Spencer Madison," he said, peeling back the foil and popping the candy in his mouth. "Remember?"

Nodding, she watched him lick dark chocolate from his thumb. How could she forget his name when he'd introduced himself shortly after claiming the seat next to hers three hours ago? Since they'd left Washington, he'd succeeded in telling her a dozen other facts about himself, too. None of which she'd asked for. All of which, surprisingly, she remembered. Especially that he would be around Follett River for the next few weeks working on his novel.

She dropped her head back on the seat. She had phone calls to make, a résumé to update and a letter of recommendation to look forward to. But right now all she wanted was to arrive quietly in the small New Jersey town, slip into the safety of her family home and lick her wounded pride until she figured out what else she had to do about the mess she was in. The last thing she needed was a distraction like Spencer Madison.

"Going home for Christmas?"

"Yes, and my ten-year high school reunion," she answered before she thought to stop herself. She slowly slid her gaze toward him. How was he managing to catch her off guard like this?

"I went to mine a few years back," he said, shaking his head and chuckling. "You're going to have a great time."

Wrong. The thought of showing up at her reunion without a date was as appealing as facing an IRS audit alone. Of course, she had no intention of dating anyone anytime soon anyway. Being dumped by her boyfriend yesterday was almost as humiliating as being fired from her Capitol Hill job the day before. Almost.

She wrapped her arms tightly around her midriff. Had she really been voted The Girl Most Likely To Succeed by her graduating class or was that just a nightmare she had last night? She winced when she thought about the disgraceful reality of her life. Nothing like this was supposed to happen. Not to Jade Macleod, the planner, the prioritizer, the achiever. The class president. Pressing back against her seat, she gave into a weary sigh.

"Hey, are you okay?" he asked, leaning close again.

She could smell orange-flavored chocolate on his breath, the expensive leather of his bomber jacket tucked between them and, most enticing of all, his clean, male scent. Her heart was pounding hard enough to make her skin tingle. For one heavenly moment she closed her eyes and escaped into the sensual haze his presence created.

What was it about this audacious stranger that she found so compelling? His voice? His scent? She squirmed in her seat. His taste in chocolate? Her growing smile suddenly froze. He was pressing his knee against her thigh with all the familiarity and intensity of a concerned lover.

Stiffening her spine she sat straight up. A lover? Who said anything about a lover? The man was a stranger. Granted, a good-looking, chocolate-scented one, but for all she knew there were other words that could describe him better. Slippery. Unstable. Dangerous.

She looked up for the emergency brake then

winced when she realized what she was considering. She was on a train to Follett River, not in a lost episode of "I Love Lucy." There was no call for histrionics.

"I'm perfectly fine," she said, hoping her cool tone and hard stare would make him move back.

He didn't move.

Honestly, he was close enough for her to count his eyelashes if they weren't so thick. She uncrossed her legs and looked away. His warm breath continued playing against her neck as subtly as a sweet caress. Shifting her weight to one hip, she adjusted the hem of her skirt then crossed her legs in the opposite direction.

"Are you sure you're fine?"

"Yes." *No!* The next two weeks of her life were going to be an endurance test for her nervous system. She was about to attend her high school reunion *without a date.* On top of that she was going to have to deal with all those questions about her illustrious career on Capitol Hill. *A career that no longer existed.* And just to make things interesting, this would all take place over the Christmas holidays. She squeezed her eyes shut. Maybe she should have pressed for an emergency appointment with that psychotherapist instead of tucking her tail between her legs and hurrying home.

Candy, even chocolate candy, couldn't fix her problems. Nor could brawny, breezy Spencer Madison. Stealing a glance at him, she suddenly felt a flicker of self-doubt tickling beneath her breastbone. Before she could figure out a logical reason for the sensation, the door at the end of the car rattled open.

"Follett River. Next stop, Follett River."

Turning away from Spencer, she pressed both hands against the window as the train crossed the bridge over Follett River. Then a stand of snow-laden pines whisked by and the college bell tower came into view. She was already picturing herself climbing into a taxi and telling the driver to take her to Red Oak Road...the back way. The last thing she needed right now was to run into a chatty friend.

"Looks like something off of a church calendar out there."

So what if *he* was leaning over her shoulder? This was the happiest she'd felt in a long time. "Yes, it does," she said, not caring if he heard the rush of excitement in her voice or saw her beaming.

After a second he backed off, leaving her to bask in the special moment. But not for long. As the train pulled into the station, the brakes grabbed and half the contents of her purse spilled onto the floor.

"No," she said, blocking him with her arm when he reached to help her. "I'll get it."

As she scrambled to pick up her things, Spencer Madison let out a heartfelt "What have we here?" followed by an amused laugh.

Jade fought feminine instinct to defend the scattered contents of her purse. What business was it of his anyway? Besides, in a matter of seconds, she would be escaping this newest distracting bid by him to engage her in conversation. She tossed a tube of lipstick back in her purse, followed by her day planner notebook and flip phone. What made him think talking would work when that smile of his hadn't? That smile...

Before she could help herself, she twisted around to look up at him. He had the whitest, most even teeth she'd ever seen. And those dimples were incredibly charming on a man she suspected was approaching his mid-thirties.

"Check that out." Jutting his thumb toward the window on the opposite side of the train car, he said, "Looks like we arrived right on time for the celebration..." He gave her a comical frown. "You never did tell me your name."

"No, I didn't," she said, purposely giving him her most sincere smile to confuse him before turning away. She didn't care to know what he was talking about. Reaching for a pen that had rolled beneath her seat, she shoved it in her purse, grabbed her coat and started up from her seat.

Outside, a band began playing "Hello, Dolly." There was something eerily familiar about the enthusiastic though amateurish rendition. Jade eased back onto her seat. Leaning across Spencer Madison's lap, she felt her eyes widening as her heart contracted. "Oh, no."

"They're a little heavy on the drums, but that kind of energy sure catches your attention, doesn't it?" Standing, Spencer Madison purposely blocked her view as he shrugged into his jacket. "I wonder who rates this kind of welcome."

She pressed back in the seat for another look, her gaze darting around him like a hummingbird. When she didn't answer him, Spencer reached to the rack above them for their luggage.

"You're getting out here, right?" he asked as several people squeezed by him on their way off the train.

Jade Macleod gave him the kind of blank look reserved for startled deer trapped in car headlights. In the three weeks Spencer Madison had been following her, she had always appeared in complete control of herself. The sight of her like this jarred him. He could almost allow himself to feel sorry for her current state, but that wouldn't get his job done.

"You sure you're okay?"

Reaching across his empty seat she took a white-knuckled grip on the armrest and scanned the scene outside.

"I—I... Oh, no, it—it ca— Ohh, *no.*"

He gently shook his head as she tried to force a coherent sentence. "Sorry," he said, with a shrug. "If you think it would help, I'd be willing to buy a vowel."

"Move!" she said, frantically grabbing onto the leather sleeve of his jacket, and pulling herself past him to the seat across the aisle. Kneeling on the cushion, she bent low to the window, sending her short skirt up her thigh.

Spencer indulged himself with an admiring glance lasting a full five seconds. He'd seen her at her health club wearing less, but this time those firm, sleek thighs were so close they were making his fingers itch.

"What is it?" he asked, pinching the bridge of his nose as he leaned down. When she started speaking in broken syllables again, he moved in close, curving his large hand around her shoulder.

"Is there someone out there you don't want to

see?'' When she didn't answer, he dipped his head lower and read from the banner outside. "Jade Macleod." Turning his face toward her profile, he felt her hair brush his cheek. "Is that your name?"

She nodded.

"Jade, you look a little pale. You're not going to pass out on me, are you?"

She twisted around on her knees to stare blankly into his eyes. A second later the tuba player took advantage of a lull and blew an amazingly rude note. The sound sent Jade forward against Spencer's chest.

"Steady there, kiddo. What's this all about?"

"It's about me," she said, pushing away from him the instant, it seemed, she came to her senses and realized she'd been burrowing into his embrace.

"Who are you?"

"Nobody anymore. I swear," she said just as the crowd outside began chanting her name.

Spence looked out the window again then gave her a squinty-eyed look. "Well, you're the most popular nobody I've ever met."

With her gaze darting nervously around them, she whipped down the window shade. The train car was empty except for the two of them. "It's too complicated to explain right now."

Holding up his hand, he brought his thumb and index finger as close as he could without actually making contact with the other. "Could you give me just a tiny hint?" he asked, hoping his attempt at humor would break the tension and calm her down.

She shook her head. Her desperate expression told him she wasn't in the mood for joking. Truth was, she looked as if she was beginning to hyperventilate.

For the first time since he'd started his investigation, he wondered if the pretty congressional aide might be more of a pawn than a perpetrator in the suspected travel fraud in her office. Stunned by his sentimental thought, he rolled his eyes. He knew nothing for certain yet. Except one thing. If anyone understood that hard-edged journalism had no place for sappy softies, it was Spencer Madison.

He gave her a skeptical look.

She pushed him into the aisle. "I need a favor."

"What kind of favor?"

"Pretend we're traveling together."

He stepped back and lowered his chin. "You want me to pretend we're, uh..." Smiling, he moved his hand back and forth between them. "Together? As in...together?"

"What?"

"In the Biblical sense together?"

"No! Not like that. I want you to pretend you're my assistant," Jade said, picking up a piece of her luggage and reaching for another. "And only if anyone asks."

"Oh," he said, his voice flat with disappointment.

She gave him a look to match the temperature and pointedness of the icicles hanging from the station's overhang. "Why am I not surprised?" she murmured under her breath.

Jade began silently counting to ten, hoping her composure would return by the time she finished. She made it to three before blurting out, "Well, can you help me?"

A subtle, indefinable light came into his eyes at the same moment a slow smile began deepening his lengthy dimples. Later, when she was safely hiding in her old room, she would take the time to curse his ancestry. "Look, I know you must find this amusing but I just need to get through that crowd out there as quickly as I can. Will you help me?"

"That depends."

"On what?"

"Will we be having dinner together afterward?"

"Dinner? Yes, yes, of course." She was willing to promise him a new car and an all-expense-paid trip to the Bahamas. Hell, she'd throw in ten pounds of Smoochies, too, if that would get him to help her.

Her heart began sinking when he glanced outside then gave her a dubious frown. Just when he had her convinced he was about to say no, he picked up his suitcases. "So, where are we going for dinner, Jade Macleod?"

A rush of relief mixed with a generous amount of gratitude filled her heart. Behind all that exasperating behavior there was a decent man! "Anywhere you want, Spencer Madison. Just get me out of here."

She followed him up the aisle to the opposite end of the train, then hung back when he motioned for her to wait. He went down the steps, set down his luggage and reached back for hers. After setting everything on the platform, he looked around then motioned her down the steps. "Watch out for my computer case."

She didn't have to. He lifted her off the bottom step and over the case before her high-heeled boots could touch the platform. The effortless, take-charge move took her breath away. An unfamiliar excitement shivered through her. He wasn't the irritating stranger anymore and she was feeling anything but weary. With his hands still curved around her waist, he leaned his head close enough to hers so she felt his beard stubble brush her cheek.

"Where to now?"

"In that door, through the station and out to the taxi stand. Then—"

"Jade! There you are," her brother shouted from down the platform.

Without missing a bone-jangling note, the members of the Follett River High School marching band promptly pivoted in her direction. Spencer took his hands away and a few seconds later the music stopped.

"Ladies and gentlemen, please welcome Representative Bloomfield's aide, valedictorian and president of her high school class and the girl voted Most Likely to Succeed—my sister, Jade Macleod."

As the small crowd whooped and clapped their hands, Neal Macleod said in a stage whisper, "I'm doing a feature for the *Follett River Ledger.* I'm calling it, 'What Ever Happened To The Girl Most Likely To Succeed?' I came up with the idea this morning over at the Chocolate Chip Café when I heard the band director say the band needed practice. Kinda nice how it all came together. What do you think?"

She stared at him in silence.

"Right. Okay," he said, sticking a small tape recorder within an inch of her lips. "So how does it feel to be back home in Follett River for your ten-year high school reunion?"

She opened her mouth. Nothing came out but a strangled rasp. Desperate, she looked up at Spencer.

Without hesitation, Spencer leaned close to the recorder. "I know Jade would like to tell you how surprised and honored she is by all of this attention. Unfortunately she's recovering from a bad case of laryngitis."

"And you are...?" Neal asked.

"Her personal assistant, Spencer Madison," he said, glancing down at her.

Personal? She never said anything about personal. Pressing her lips together, she looked first at Spencer and then at her brother. The good news was, she didn't have to choose; she could murder the both of them and the punishment would be the same.

"Jade, you have your own personal assistant now," Neal said, as he reached across to shake Spencer's hand, "I *am* impressed."

And you're lying, too, little brother. She could tell by the look in Neal's eyes that his incredibly intelligent mind was in overdrive, trying to figure out what she was doing with Spencer.

She wondered that herself. In her haste to avoid public embarrassment, she hadn't considered that Spencer Madison was all wrong to play her assistant. While she had shown up in her business suit, he was standing beside her in a leather bomber jacket, jeans that molded to everything and two-days' worth of beard stubble that would have appeared contrived under the best circumstances. She swallowed slowly. She was already regretting her hasty decision.

"Smile," someone shouted.

And Spencer did just that. His grin was genuine, his attitude—pleased-to-be-here—and his white teeth the envy of any politician. Down-to-earth yet dazzling, Jade couldn't take her eyes from him. No one else could, either.

"You're not smiling," he said without moving his lips.

He was right. She'd been too busy staring at his born-to-break-hearts smile. Not *her* heart, of course, she thought as she turned away from him to smile at the camera. A second later her gaze strayed back to him as he gave a thumbs-up to the crowd.

They whooped their approval.

She gave him a light kick on the ankle. Honestly, what some people wouldn't do for a free meal.

"All right." Spencer clapped his hands together once then turned to Neal. "She should probably get home and rest."

"Rough day?" Neal asked, pocketing his tape recorder.

"Rough," Spencer agreed. "We worked right up until it was time to catch our train."

We? Our? Would this madness ever end? The two men reached for the luggage as she turned on her heel and started toward the parking lot. The band followed them, blasting out "Moon River" this time.

Jade's heart was already sinking when she spotted the hand-lettered sign attached to Neal's car. Welcome Home, Congressional Aide Jade Macleod. Climbing in the back seat, she quickly slammed the door.

True, Spencer Madison had done what she'd asked. He also proved he could think quickly on his feet. But did he have to look so damned pleased with himself while he did it? Well, he could eat worms for dinner for all she cared. And he could eat them alone.

Reaching for the door lock, she jammed down the button. At that same moment the front car doors opened.

"Hey, sis, I'll head out to the house first to drop you off," Neal said, as he and his photographer climbed in. "Then I've got to get Casey and me back to the paper so I can have a look at these photos."

Before Jade could respond, the back door opposite hers opened. "Moon River" was blaring into the car's interior as Spencer Madison got in. His surprise entry had her lurching forward and reaching for her brother's shoulder.

Without missing a beat, Neal continued. "Spencer said he was going to be staying over at the Maxwell, but I told him living in a hotel was crazy when we have all that room at the house. When he told me you two are working on that special project together, I said it only makes sense that you both should be near each other."

Jade's mouth dropped open as she turned to glare at Spencer. "What project?" she mouthed silently.

"That's okay," Spence said in a perfectly audible voice. "I haven't mentioned the nature of Representative Bloomfield's project." He pressed a finger to his lips. "It's still secret."

Secret project? There was no secret project, she wanted to shout. But she couldn't now that Casey was sitting in the front seat next to Neal. The fewer people that knew about this catastrophe, the better.

She slumped back in her seat as Neal tooted his horn then waved off the high school band that was circling the car. "Moon River" suddenly ended as the band members scattered out of the way.

"Their particular interpretation needs a tad more work," Neal said as he started the car. Spencer and Casey agreed, as he turned on the radio and drove off. Channel surfing, he quickly landed on a station playing reggae music. "Yesss." He turned up the volume. "Now *that's* music."

Jade checked her watch then inched closer to her door.

Without hesitation, Spencer stretched his arm over the back of her seat and leaned in close to her ear. "How'd I do?" he asked, his leg casually pressing against hers.

"Let's put it this way. No matter what my brother promised, you're not moving in with us. And you can forget about dinner," she whispered, giving his knee a hearty shove. Hard muscle and bone bounced back against her own. "Get off me!" she seethed, thumping him harder this time.

Neal took that moment to glance in the rearview mirror. "Settle down back there, you kids," he said, in his best imitation of their father's voice. "Or, I swear, I'm turning this car around and we're all going home."

Coming off the seat, Jade grabbed onto her brother's headrest and opened her mouth to speak. Casey took that moment to snap off a few more photos, momentarily blinding her with the flash.

"Thought I'd finish the roll," she heard the girl say.

"Uh, uh," Neal said, waving his finger in the air between the spots of light. "You'd better save that voice, sis. Mom and Dad are at the house waiting to hear all about how you're straightening out those naughty politicians on Capitol Hill.''

Sinking back in her seat, she gave a whimper that was lost to everyone but Spencer in the reggae din. If they only knew how naughty.

"Don't worry," Spencer said, patting her shoulder. "I can get you through that, too."

Two

"One night," Jade said as she paced inside the west-wing bedroom, her fingers firmly pressed to her temples. "I can manage this for one night. All I have to do is come up with a logical explanation for getting rid of you tomorrow. Early." She motioned emphatically with both hands. "Very early.

"In the meantime, you're going to have to do exactly as I say. You're not to go downstairs without me. You're not to speak to anyone without me. And—"

"Nice place," Spencer said, cutting her off with enough over-the-top enthusiasm to let her know he was not talking about the Hotel Maxwell.

Pointedly ignoring him, she went on. "And if I can figure out a good excuse for you to eat dinner up here, you're going to—"

She froze in her tracks when he let loose with a long, spirited whistle. "What is it now?"

"Did you do that?" he asked, as he removed his wallet and tossed it on the bedside table.

Her annoyance was building with each heartbeat. If Spencer Madison was running for the Most Aggravating Person of the Year Award, she'd vote twice for him. She took a labored breath then let it out through her nose. "Did I do what?"

Shaking his head with genuine appreciation, he stared up at the hand-painted bluebirds and pink ribbons on the ceiling. "The mural."

"And what if I did?"

"It's damn good."

"Oh." She squinted upward and then at him. "You really think so?"

"Absolutely. The gold on the ribbons and the clouds in the background give it a kind of surrealistic feel. "When did you paint it?"

"The summer I turned sixteen." Recalling that carefree period in her life, she laughed softly. "I was heavily influenced by Disney cartoons back then. And anything remotely French and romantic—" She stopped in midsentence when she realized he was trying to steer her off the subject of getting rid of him. Scowling, she clamped both hands on her hips.

Controlling Spencer Madison for the next twelve hours wasn't going to be easy, but she wasn't giving up. "Have you been listening to anything I've said?"

Carefully removing several shirts from his suitcase, Spencer set the stack on the bed. "I haven't missed a word."

"Okay," she said, challenging him with a jut of her chin. "What did I say?"

He reached for his shaving kit. "Let's see," he said, tossing it back and forth between his hands before pausing thoughtfully. "You've been heavily influenced by anything remotely French and romantic—"

"Before that."

"You mean, downstairs just now with your parents? Don't worry. You were very good," he said, winking at her.

"What was that wink for?"

"I think they like me."

Jade flew across the room. "Obviously you have *not* been listening. You're here for one night and one night only so there'll be no need to unpack," she said, scooping up his shirts then dropping the armload back into his suitcase. She was on home ground now. In a place where she felt safe and confident, and he was not going to change that with a wink, that chipper talk or his good ol' boy attitude.

Rezipping the luggage, she shoved it off the bed. "And just because my parents offered you good brandy, doesn't mean they like you. They do that to everyone I bring home."

When he looked as if he was going to reach for the phone, she lunged to push it to the other side of the night table. "You have not lucked into a meal ticket here so don't even think about canceling your reservations at the Maxwell."

He studied her for a moment then slipped his hands in his pockets and nonchalantly leaned around her for a look at the balcony doors. She took that opportunity to snatch his wallet from the night table.

"Look at me," she said, shaking the leather trifold at him. "I'm locking this in my father's office safe downstairs, so don't get any crazy ideas about robbing us then sneaking out. And I'm counting the silver and checking your bags before you leave here, too."

As his roving gaze landed on her again, he took a step closer, bumping the toes of his loafers against her pumps. His towering height caused her to look up instead of down. One deep breath and his chest would be pressing against her breasts. She swallowed carefully.

He lowered his chin. "You mean you'd like to go through my personal possessions?"

Suddenly the spacious room she'd spent her childhood in felt claustrophobically small. She had all she could do not to cup her fingers over his stubbly beard and hold him...back. Along with his serious expression, his masculine stance took her breath away. Maybe that terrorist-cum-movie star look wasn't as repulsive as she once thought. "I—I didn't say that."

He moved closer. "You didn't have to," he said, his voice rumbling through her like soft thunder on a sultry afternoon.

Her eyelids fluttered shut. He was going to kiss her. The kind of hot and thorough kiss that left you breathless and achy. The kind that made you moan for more. The kind she'd read about but never experienced. Tingling sensations were scattering through her body like blind butterflies on too much caffeine. Lifting her chin, she allowed her lips to flower open. Any second now he was—

She heard him sit down on the bed.

Of course he wasn't going to kiss her. Dropping her chin, she kept her eyelids tightly shut as the words from a popular serenity prayer rolled through her mind. After a moment she opened her eyes, slapped his wallet on the table and looked down at him with condescension worthy of royalty. "I know what this is about now."

He gave the mattress a few test bounces without bothering to look up at her. "What?"

"You're trying to turn this side trip into a research experiment for that novel you're writing, aren't you?" Before he could answer, she went on. "Well, you won't be around here long enough to get anywhere with that idea, so don't bother fluffing the pillows. And stop that bouncing! This sleigh bed's an antique. Did you hear me?"

When she grabbed his knees to steady him, their noses brushed. Startled by the playful yet intimate contact with him, she stopped moving.

He smiled. "This was your bed when you were little, right?"

Letting go of his knees, she pulled back. "How do you know that?"

"Easy. Quality piece," he said, running his hand along an inviting turn of wood. "Nice, solid curves." Dropping back on the white-on-white, pin-striped comforter, he opened his arms and wriggled his hips. "Makes a little noise when it's shaken…kinda reminds me of you."

She brought her fists straight down to her sides. "I am not laughing."

He kicked off his shoes, swung his legs onto the bed and folded his arms behind his head. "I know, but I am a patient man," he said, easing back onto the bank of ruffly, white eyelet pillow shams.

Avoiding his out-there-and-in-your-face expression, Jade dropped her frosty gaze over all six feet plus of him. Stretching, sprawling...standing, breathing; it didn't matter. She'd never met anyone more comfortable with his own body. From the short time she'd known him, she was certain that Spencer Madison would be just as comfortable stretched out on that bed in his birthday suit.

The breath-stealing image appeared out of nowhere, bolting her to the floor. All those strong lines and angles of inviting masculinity contrasting with the soft, white comforter...*her* soft, white comforter. A wave of body heat swept through her, singeing her flesh. If her face was half as red as the rest of her body felt, he was going to know in an instant what she was thinking. She willed her eyes to look away, but when that didn't happen she rubbed at her forehead.

"Headache?"

She slowly lowered her hands. Something ached, but it wasn't her head.

"What's wrong?" he asked, curling his torso up and toward her. Leaning on his elbow, he patted the mattress. "Did you want to sleep here tonight?"

There? She swallowed. *Right there in that warm spot? Where you rested your head on the pillow? Where you opened your arms and wriggled your hips? Where I pictured your naked body?* "Not anymore," she said, as she headed for the connecting door to the next room.

"Jade. Hold on a minute."

From the corner of her eye, she could see him swinging his legs off the bed and planting his feet on the pale pink rug.

"Why are you doing this? What are you up to?"

"I'm making it clear to you that you're leaving here as soon as I can manage it, and with as little fanfare as possible."

"That's not what I meant," he said, angling his head in gentle reprimand.

She gave a huffy, impatient sigh. "Don't you have plans to be with your family for the holidays?"

"Not this year. They're on a cruise somewhere in the Caribbean." He pushed up onto his feet. "What are you trying to hide, Jade?"

She slowed her steps as a tiny alarm bell jangled in her head. Was that genuine concern she heard? Or was he setting her up again to play another exasperating game of cat and mouse? Either way, it didn't matter. She'd been through enough humiliation in the last few days to last a lifetime. And until she received that promised letter of recommendation from Sylvia Bloomfield so that she could move on finding another job, she didn't need Spencer Madison around distracting her. On any level. "It's none of your—"

"It is now."

She could tell by the way he cut her off that Spencer Madison wasn't about to back down. He had time on his side, too; he wasn't going anywhere until breakfast. Sighing, she ran her tongue back and forth

over the edges of her teeth. What had she expected?
She knew he would ask this question sooner or later.
She also knew she owed him some sort of an explanation, too. But that didn't make it any easier to come
up with an answer.

"Well?" He raised a brow.

Reaching to tuck a lock of hair behind her ear, she
studied him carefully. He'd been sending her mixed
signals since the first time he'd brushed against her.
What he meant, what he wanted and who he was were
as unknown to her as her own future. No way was
she going to tell him that she'd just been fired when
she couldn't bring herself to admit it to anyone else.
Not even her own family. There was only one thing
to do. Since she was the world's worst liar, she'd have
to offer him an altered version of the lesser of two
evil truths.

"My boyfriend was supposed to have come on this
trip, but we had this disagreement…this big, and…
well, *personal* disagreement. It couldn't have happened at a worse time, I know, yet I still found it
necessary to break up with him." She was starting to
ramble, but she always did that when she lied.

Spencer's face contorted to a sympathetic frown.
Too sympathetic. But there was no going back now,
so she went on, effusing her explanation with a whine
worthy enough to win an Academy Award. "I really
can't explain why I panicked this afternoon. Probably
the stress of the breakup. I mean, it wasn't easy after
all the time I put into the relationship, and when
he—"

"Bull."

"Bull?" One hand shot to her hip and the other

snapped toward him with the efficiency and speed of a karate chop. "What's that supposed to mean?"

"That means, I don't believe you."

"You think this trip isn't embarrassing for me? My parents have been hounding me to bring Richard for a visit. And at the last minute he's a no-show. Believe me," she said, pointing a thumb over her shoulder and toward the door, "they haven't started their main interrogation session yet.

"And in case you've forgotten, I'm facing having to attend my high school reunion alone. Not that it means anything to you, but I, the girl voted Most Likely to Succeed, am not looking forward to dancing with myself at that affair."

"That's what's got you coming off your spool?" He shook his head. "I don't think so."

"Why you insufferable, obnoxious, sanctimonious, know-it-all, you don't know anything about me."

"Hold on, hold on," Spencer said, raising his hands in surrender. "You're right. I don't know you and you don't know me, but maybe that can work to your advantage."

She reached for the doorknob.

"Jade, please. Hear me out," Spencer said, working to gain her trust with the most concerned tone he could muster. A journalistic strategem he'd practiced for the better part of seven years. He took a few steps toward her. "We both know there's a lot more to this than what you've told me. Whatever it is, you're going to feel a lot better once you talk about it."

She looked cautiously over her shoulder at him. He took it as his cue to continue.

"You know, sometimes a stranger can be a better

listener than a friend or a family member. With a stranger, there's no history, no expectations, no emotional connection to the person or the problem." Shoving his hands in his pockets, he arched a brow. "If you're ready to talk, I'm willing to listen."

Spence watched as she stared at the lush weeping fig tree by the balcony doors for a long moment, then blew a puff of air through her lips. She was coming around. He shifted his weight from one foot to the other. It was all he could do not to reach for his tape recorder.

"Okay. I'll tell you the truth, but you're not to go blabbing this."

He made a zipping motion across his lips.

"Richard left *me*."

This little gem was a far cry from what he'd expected: an admission that she'd been fired from her Capitol Hill job, an angry burst of information on Representative Sylvia Bloomfield and maybe even a confession of her own involvement in the travel fraud he was investigating.

He stroked his stubbly beard and smiled to himself. He was an optimistic man; he'd try again later about her job. In the meantime, and not that he gave a rat's aorta, but just how important was this damn boyfriend to her? With that red hair, those big blue eyes and that gorgeous body, Jade Macleod went way beyond pretty and well into the realm of beautiful. What kind of a fool would walk out on her?

"You sound more ticked off than hurt."

"I can assure you, I am hurt. In fact, I—I'm devastated. Humiliated." She blinked several times, trying, he guessed, to produce a tear or two. When that didn't work, she pressed her lips together and looked away. "I think it's made me a little crazy."

He liked the way she held herself together. He liked the way she fell apart, too. But when she tried to lie, he had to bite back a smile. Wringing her hands, Jade chattered on about her broken heart as her beautiful blue-eyed gaze darted around the room. So much wasted energy. He could think of better ways to channel it.

Resisting the urge to adjust his inseam, Spence pinched the bridge of his nose instead. Enough of this sentimental, sexy, screwball nonsense. What the hell was he thinking about? He was here for one thing. Information for a no-nonsense, hard-facts exposé on Jade Macleod's ex-boss. *Let the games begin,* he thought as he held up his hand for her to stop.

"Clear up a point for me, will you?" he asked as he walked over and handed her his handkerchief. "You said your parents have never met Richard."

Sniffing, she eyed him suspiciously. "That's right."

"Well, wouldn't it have made more sense if you'd asked me to pretend to be him instead of your assistant?"

She stared at him blankly.

"It's none of my business, but he must not have been very good in the—"

She leveled a finger and a warning look at him. "Watch it."

"Hey, all I'm saying is, if you're not bothering to replace him, there must not have been much of a relationship to replace."

"There's more to a relationship than...well... that," she said as her face reddened. "Besides, I only needed you to pretend at the train station. Things were never supposed to go this far." Raising the handkerchief, she turned away to blow her nose.

"Whatever. It just sounds to me as if you're more interested in what people think of your career than your love life. Am I right?"

Balling the handkerchief, she shoved it back in his hand. "You're really enjoying this, aren't you?"

"Hmm?" He stuffed the handkerchief into his pocket.

"This psychological ploy to get me to talk about myself so you'll have something to chew on for that novel. What's the matter, Spence? Suffering from the proverbial writer's block? Are you a little weak on plot? Short on characterization? Is there fizzle where there should be zing?"

He didn't bother hiding his smile as he backed away. "*Is* there fizzle where there should be zing?" Picking up his suitcase, he placed it on the bed again. "I'll let you know as soon as I find out. Oh, by the way. Dinner with your family tonight doesn't count. You still owe me one."

"It certainly does count. I have no intention of being seen with you in public. The fewer people I have to explain you to, the better," she said, reaching behind her for the doorknob and twisting it open. "What's that smile for?"

"In case you've forgotten, we've already been seen in public. And what are you going to say when people read about us in their newspapers?"

"Do I look worried?"

She did, but considering the daggers he was already dodging, he decided not to answer.

"Well, I'm not." She was rubbing her temples again. "This all comes under the heading of damage control, which is something of a specialty of mine."

Spence felt his ears perk up. "Really?"

"Maybe. Anyway, much as I love my brother, he will never meet his deadline because, unfortunately, Neal's never finished anything in his life. Now, if you don't mind," she said, heading back to the hall door for her suitcases, "I'm going to settle in. I'll be back for you later."

When he made a move to help, she waved him off. "Don't touch them," she said, grabbing the suitcases from his reach and heading for the connecting door to the next bedroom. "Don't go anywhere, don't talk to anyone and don't use the phone unless you have your own calling card."

Before he could respond, she kicked the door shut behind her.

Where was he! Jade knocked for the third time.

She hadn't meant to leave him alone this long, but somehow her intended five-minute nap had raged out of control. Now two hours had disappeared and so, it seemed, had Spencer Madison.

She called his name through the closed door. No answer. Frowning, she pushed it open, poked her head in and looked around. His wallet was right where she'd left it. Casting a quick glance toward the hall door, she slipped into the room and headed for the night table. The temptation to look through the brown leather trifold gnawed at her insides like a hungry pit bull puppy. She rubbed her moist palms against the tunic top of her black evening pajamas. Everything she'd been taught about right and wrong was fast-forwarding through her mind.

If ever there was a reason to break a rule, Spencer Madison's presence was it. She had a right—no, a duty—to check him out. Switching on the lamp, she picked up his wallet and began unfolding it.

"Can I help you find something?"

The sound of his voice had the same effect on her as a minor earthquake. Slamming the wallet back onto the table, she accidentally sent the lamp crashing sideways onto the bed. When she scrambled to right it, her knee connected with the corner of the night table.

"No. I was doing just fine," she said, rubbing her knee as she turned toward him. He was lounging in the doorway, his arms crossed, his one shoulder casually pressed against the door frame. "Do you always sneak up on people like that?"

"Yes. Do you always go through your guest's belongings?"

"You're not a guest," she said, reaching behind her to stop the drawer handle from rattling.

"Don't tell that to your parents," he said as a lazy grin lit his face. "They've laid out quite a spread down there. Why don't you come on down and see?"

"I thought we agreed that you were going to stay up here until I came to get you. I don't appreciate you wandering around my house," she said, crossing the room to where he blocked the doorway.

"After I made some phone calls to let people know where I'd be, things got pretty boring. By the way,

I'm short on hangers in my closet. Think you could lend me some?''

"You don't need hangers because you're not staying.''

"Why not? We were doing so well.''

"You were doing so well, but I'm not like you. I dislike taking advantage of people. I hate lying. And I especially hate lying to people I love. I'm going down there now," she said, turning sideways to shimmy past him. She hurried toward the stairs then paused at the top step to turn and face him again. "I'm going to tell them all about this ridiculous mistake I've made," she said, grasping the rail. "Then Neal will drive you into town and we can put all of this behind us.''

Spencer slowly shook his head.

"What?''

"It's not a good time for that.''

"It's as good a time as any because sooner or later they'll have to know that I've been…'' She'd almost said fired. What got into her every time she spoke to this man? His easygoing, confident manner pulled the truth right out of her. If she didn't watch herself, she'd be blurting out the whole, tawdry story of how she'd lost her job.

"Don't stop now. Let it out," he said, joining her at the top of the curved staircase.

"Okay. Dumped. I've been dumped by my boyfriend." *Just before he emptied my bank account and "borrowed" my car.* She stared hard, daring him to smile. "Are you happy now?" Spencer looked disappointed. But not for long.

"Mildly perplexed. Look, I could be wrong, but I don't think you'll be bringing any of this up tonight."

"Well, I'm not interested in what you think. This is a personal matter," she said, continuing down the stairs. "I made two mistakes. I allowed myself to panic. And I involved you. I'm not making a third one by keeping this charade going any longer."

He followed her across the tiled foyer toward a set of oak doors. "What charade are you talking about?"

For a scary moment, she had the feeling he was referring to her firing. But he couldn't know that because nobody knew yet except Sylvia Bloomfield and her. They'd both agreed that the announcement would be quietly made after the holidays.

She closed her hand over the shiny brass door lever. "Don't be cute. All you have to concern yourself with is that you're getting the meal I promised you, eating it quickly and getting back upstairs to repack. You're leaving here tonight. It's a done deal, Spence."

His growing smile sent a shiver of suspicion through her.

"Did you ever notice that things are never as simple as they seem?" he asked, sauntering toward her.

"As far as you're concerned, they are."

"What's your big hurry?"

"Look. All along I've planned to spend a quiet holiday with my family. Alone. Without strangers."

"Flexibility is a highly underrated virtue."

She narrowed her eyes as he wrapped his hand around the brass lever next to hers and smiled. What was he up to now? They pushed opened the double doors.

From all parts of the room came a rousing chorus of "Surprise!"

Three

Twelve hours, too many half-truths and one champagne hangover later, Jade walked into the Chocolate Chip Café. Mouthwatering aromas of gourmet coffees and homemade desserts were mixing with the snow-scented air that blew in with her.

Smiling to herself, she closed the door then looked around her old high school hangout, now a successful college coffee-and-dessert bar owned by a former classmate. Behind the counter, Megan Sloan managed to return her wave between twisting knobs and flipping levers on the cappuccino machine. The whooshing sounds added to the background hum of conversation in the sun-filled room. Her friend had made several changes to the place yet managed to retain the fun feeling that still made it one of Jade's favorite places in Follett River.

As she shrugged out of her coat, the bell above the door jingled, signaling someone else's arrival. She looked over her shoulder at a smiling Spencer.

"No dents," he said, referring to the car he'd just parked.

"Considering the way you drive," she murmured, "that could start me believing in Christmas miracles."

But she wasn't thinking about Christmas or miracles. She was reminiscing about the old days when the place reeked of greasy burgers, industrial-strength hair spray and teen spirit. Behind her, Spencer was stomping snow from his shoes and unzipping his bomber jacket. Surprisingly, his sounds were blending with her cherished memories. The nostalgic moment wrapped itself around her heart, making her smile.

For about two seconds.

Suddenly Spencer opened his arms, closed his eyes and pulled in a deep, noisy breath. The grand movement jolted her out of her memories and back to reality.

"Ahh. I love the smell of cappuccino in the morning."

His dramatic delivery sent four nearby coeds into a table huddle and a frantic flurry of whispers.

Jade winced. She had yet to go anywhere with Spencer that he didn't attract attention. She turned to give him a disapproving look but ended up tapping her toe on the floor. With his eyes still closed, she could only stare and wait for him to open them.

Several seconds later she was still staring. From his sybaritic smile to the snug fit of his jeans, there was no way any female in a hundred-yard radius could not stare. He was a startlingly handsome man.

Casually brushing at her bangs, she managed a peek toward the coeds. With the thumbs-up and appreciative smiles they were sending her way, the girls appeared to be in wholehearted agreement.

She responded with a weak smile then turned around to face Spencer. "When you're done emoting, you can hang up my coat," she said, shoving it against the solid wall of his chest.

She reached around him to shut the door but he was faster. His move brought his face inches away from hers.

"Are you still mad at your mother because she insisted I drive her car?" he asked, his fingers covering hers in a warm caress.

"I'm not mad at my mother. Unlike you, I know exactly what she's up to."

He tilted his head. "And what's that?"

"I'll give you a hint. Last time I brought someone home, she tried to throw us a surprise wedding."

Beneath her hand, Jade could feel soft laughter rumbling in his chest. An odd tickling sensation started deep in her own. She started to smile, but stopped the instant she realized her defenses were dropping away. Why had she told him *that*? Was he laughing at her? Or was he laughing with her? Drawing her hand away, she let him know by a quick change in her expression that she was through with their bantering.

"What is her favorite color, by the way?"

"Teal," she said, lifting a newspaper from a stack

near the door. Creasing it with a snapping sound, she tucked it under her arm. "Why?"

"I overheard her and your father discussing what to get me for Christmas. I was hoping you'd give me a few suggestions for what to buy them."

"No. Don't even think about it. You'll only be encouraging them. Besides, I didn't bring you here to talk about Christmas shopping. I have a much more serious subject to discuss."

"Uh, oh. So this is to be my farewell breakfast before I'm exiled to the Hotel Maxwell?"

"You already had breakfast. And you know as well as I do that you can't leave me now."

"Why not?" he asked, as he brushed a few drops of melted snow from the top of his head.

"Because that fan club you started amassing at the train station yesterday and continued amassing at last night's party would demand an explanation as to why my assistant moved out on me. And I can't think of one."

"Hmm. Sounds like a valid argument for us to stick together." His sympathetic expression would have convinced most people that he was concerned for her situation.

But Jade wasn't one of them.

"Look," she said, tapping her finger on the center of his chest. "You might as well know what I think of your presence in my life. You're as welcome in it as a sharp stone in my shoe. Fingernails on a chalkboard. A paper cut. But as long as you'll be leeching off my family, you and I are going to have to agree to a few ground rules. I've made a list of—"

"Gotcha."

"No," she said, jamming her finger a little harder against his colorful pullover. "I don't think you do. I have a reputation to protect, and thus far your behavior has been borderline at best. Those two facts aren't mixing well."

He moved to hang her coat over a sturdy hook. "You mean, you're concerned that I could do something that would get back to Sylvia Bloomfield and put your job in jeopardy? Maybe damage her image and your career?"

Jade's mouth went dry when she tried to swallow. "Something like that," she mumbled, as she fixed her gaze on the Santa Claus and reindeer stenciled across the café's bay window. Spencer had an uncanny talent for catching her off guard, then scaring the heck out of her when she least expected it.

Spencer patted her softly on her cheek. "You worry too much, kiddo."

The spur-of-the-moment touch was just what she needed. Thoughtful, tender, and the first sincere gesture from him that she could remember. And because of those things, his unanticipated tenderness was also just what she didn't need. Her nerves were near the snapping point. Breaking into tears moments before she planned to tell Spencer what was expected of him would not be wise. She brushed his hand away. "Don't patronize me."

"I mean it. Not everyone has parents as proud of their kid as yours. Last night I thought your dad was going to start crying along with your mother when your girlfriends started in about what a shining example you've always been to them. Even the mayor couldn't say enough about you. And when that question came up concerning the whereabouts of your absent boyfriend, everyone was extremely sympathetic.''

Clenching her fists, she fought to contain a growl, then turned and headed for a table in the back corner of the café.

Spencer hung up his jacket then followed her. As he pulled out the chair next to hers, Jade dropped her leather bag on the seat. He shrugged then moved to the one directly across from hers. ''What's the matter?''

''I was perfectly capable of explaining Richard's absence without you butting in,'' she said, dropping the newspaper on the table.

''No, you weren't. Your face got so red when your friend Rebecca asked you about him, I thought you were going to have a stroke.''

''I thought I was, too,'' she said, taking her chair then riffling through her bag for a pen and pad. ''But not until you said he was in the hospital donating a kidney to his brother. Where do you come up with these things?''

''I'm a writer.'' He smiled. ''A writer who badly needs another kick of caffeine this morning. You, on the other hand, look as if you could use a decaf.''

''That I could,'' she said, slapping a pen on the table as he started away. ''Wait. You don't know what I like or how I like it.''

''I don't? We'll see about that,'' he said, his devilish grin sending a pleasurable tickle straight up her thighs and deep into her belly.

As he walked away, she forgot about looking for her pad of paper and looked at him instead. His con-

through the front section. As he arrived at the table, she managed to fold back the paper to the editorial page.

"Caffe latte, boss lady. Extra chocolate shavings on top."

She looked up from the paper and then at him.

He pulsed one brow. "What's the matter? Isn't this what you always get?"

"Yes." She gave him a brittle smile then reached for the cup. "How did you—" she began, then broke off with a shake of her head.

Megan's coffee menu, written out in a feminine script on the board beside the counter, listed at least fifteen variations of popular coffee-bar drinks. How Spencer had managed to select not only her favorite but to know about the extra chocolate shavings she always ordered gave her the willies. Then suddenly it all made sense.

"Megan told you. Right?"

"Did she?" he asked, taking the chair opposite hers.

"Don't be funny. Thank you."

"You're welcome. Think we could call a truce here until we finish these?"

Maybe that wouldn't be such a bad idea. He'd been on good behavior for at least five minutes and she wanted him to stay that way when she had her talk with him. She watched as he took a sip, then licked the creamy foam and melted chocolate from the corner of his mouth.

"Sure," she said, holding his gaze.

"Megan said she'd be over as soon as she had a minute."

He had this staring thing down to an art. She nodded. "Great."

He nodded back.

She felt a nervous twitch of a smile tugging at her mouth. This moment of normalcy didn't have to be difficult just because it was their first one. She felt the twitch again. Good Lord, her cheeks were warming, too. This was starting to feel like a first date. She blinked and looked down.

"Here. Have some of this," she said, sliding the second section of the *Follett River Ledger* across the table. "I'm reading 'The Mad Man' column. You know, that political satirist in Washington who prefers to work anonymously. He's on vacation for a few weeks and they're reprinting some of his most popular pieces," she said, gluing her gaze to the page. "Or maybe I should say, his more controversial ones."

Spencer coughed in the middle of a swallow, then noisily cleared his throat. "You, uh, read him a lot?"

She looked up at him again. "Sure. Whether he's spicing up my own political views or simply irritating me, I never miss his column. 'The Mad Man' is a hard habit to break. He's become my shot of Tabasco in the morning."

"I've never heard him described that way before."

Leaning forward, she lowered her forearms to the table. "With all this work you've been doing on your novel, you still take time to read his column?"

"Oh, yeah. I never miss it."

"Do you ever wonder who he is? I mean, that photo of him with the goofy baseball cap pulled down over his face, he could be…anyone."

"Yeah, sometimes I wonder who he is myself." Spencer twisted his cup in a circle on its saucer then shoved his fingers through his hair. "I guess he must have had your boss squirming last month when he named her in that column on questionable political fund-raising junkets."

Jade felt the blood draining from her face. This was exactly the kind of remark she was afraid Spencer might casually make in front of a group of people. Thank God there was no one close by to hear and question her about it. She did not want to be put in a position where she had to publicly defend Sylvia Bloomfield's character. Jade repositioned herself in the cane-back chair.

True, the woman had given Jade the coveted position of congressional aide. During the past three years the job had proven to be everything she'd dreamed it would. Exciting, creative and highly satisfying. But since last Saturday, when she'd walked in on Sylvia and her assistant Lance, on top of her desk, Jade was trying hard not to think about the woman. "The Mad Man was way off the mark on that one," she said curtly.

"Was he?" Spencer asked, his gaze riveted to hers. "Some of the questions the Mad Man raised were never addressed."

"That's because they didn't warrant a response. I can assure you that Sylvia's fund-raising record is spotless."

When she couldn't tear her gaze from his, Jade raised the newspaper between them. Her heart was hammering. Even though her work consisted of legislative research, as far as Jade knew, Sylvia's fund-raising record *was* spotless. But after what she stumbled in on last Saturday, nothing she found out about the married congresswoman would surprise her.

"You're quick to defend her," Spencer said as his fingers appeared over the top of the paper. He crumpled down the edge to eye level. "And that's great to hear, because if I'm going to continue being her aide's personal assistant, I need to know Bloomfield's a respectable member of Congress."

Here we go again, she thought, as a dull ache began in her temples. "Are you through with your latte? Because I'm through with mine," she said, sliding the cup aside. Without waiting for him to respond, she went on.

"Here's the deal. You came to Follett River to work on your novel. Right?"

"Right. But who knew I'd be meeting such terrific people?"

"Who cares? These terrific people you've met are my friends. Not yours. They're only being nice to you because you're with me. Are you sure you don't have someplace else to go?" She felt her face brightening with surprise. "I could say you had a family emergency."

"I can't leave," he said with a simple shake of his head.

"Then promise me you'll stay in your room and work. And not hang around me looking for opportunistic moments to embarrass me." She leaned across the table as Megan approached. "Do you understand?" she asked in a whisper. "Room and board and leave me alone."

"Ah, here's Megan," he said, standing to pull out a chair for the pretty blond widow.

"No thanks, Spence." She looked toward Jade. "That party your parents gave last night was the most fun I've had in a long time. I only hope our high school reunion will turn out as well."

"It will be a major success because you're in charge," Jade said as she eased back in her chair. "And Rebecca Barnett's coming, so there's a double guarantee that it's going to be fun."

"I guess I've got a case of the last-minute jitters, but I shouldn't. We're all old friends." She looked at Spence then back to Jade. "Or will be soon. You have a treasure here," Megan said, patting him on the shoulder.

"Treasure?"

"Yes. Didn't Spence tell you he's volunteered to help with the reunion?"

"I was just about to do that," Spence said, as he smiled across the table at Jade.

"It'll be fun," Megan promised as she made her way back to the counter.

Jade sagged in her seat. A few minutes away from her and Spencer had finagled a way into the reunion. She shook her head. Why was she surprised? It was her own fault. She'd allowed Spencer Madison to slip into her life, and like a bead of mercury on a downhill roll, she'd been trying unsuccessfully to control him ever since.

Taking a deep breath, she held it until spots started before her eyes. She wasn't giving up. Grabbing the edge of the table, she stared him hard in the eyes as she quietly announced, "Get this straight. You're going with me to decorate and to the reunion."

"Are you on the decorating committee, too?"

"I am now."

"I can deal with that."

"Did you bring a suit with you?"

"No."

"Then you'll have to buy one. *I'm* picking it out."

"Forty-two long. Stay away from brown if you can."

"I always do. We're going down the street to Mr. Jordan's for it. Together."

"I hope we're done by one o'clock," he said, looking at his watch. "Neal and I have a basketball game planned. And then I have some shopping of my own to do. In case you've forgotten, it's Christmas Eve."

Smiling, she pretended not to hear him. "That beard will have to go."

He rubbed it thoughtfully, then shrugged. "Okay."

"And since you *are* my *personal* assistant," she said, pulling a slip of paper from her bag and fluttering it between then, "then, by all means, go forth and assist."

Spencer reached for the paper. "What's this?" he asked, glancing at the list.

"Read it," she said, crossing her arms in front of her then leaning them on the table. She smiled. "Go ahead. I want to make sure you can understand my writing."

He began reading it aloud. "'One copy of the *Washington Herald*. Two rolls of red foil wrapping paper with matching gift tags. Two bags of Smoochies. One with orange centers, one with cherry.

And one box of tamp—'" His gaze shot over the list to meet hers.

Coughing softly, he narrowed his eyes.

He'd taken a bullet in Baghdad. Come down with that strange fever in Africa. And had been declared persona non grata by at least two foreign governments. Buying feminine hygiene products in small-town America wasn't going to do him in. He could meet this challenge. "'And one box of tampons.'"

If she was disappointed by his lack of embarrassment, she didn't show it.

"Torkle's Pharmacy is two doors to the left. That way," she said, pointing up the street. "Meet me back here in fifteen minutes. I want to talk to Megan about the reunion. Alone."

Spencer gave her a spiffy salute as he stood up. "Mission accepted," he said, then waited for her smile to widen a tiny bit more. He pretended to start for the front door, then turned back, his index finger raised. If she wanted to play tit for tat, she'd met her match.

"By the way, you had a phone call this morning while you were in the shower."

Her smile froze, then melted away. "A phone call?"

"Yes. I was talking with my editor when a call-waiting came through."

"From who?"

"Let me think," he said, watching her coming slowly off her chair. "I think it was a guy...." he said, touching his forehead.

"My car," Jade whispered to herself. She never expected to see her money again, but maybe Richard realized how easy it would be for law enforcement to track the license plate on her car. "Was it Richard?"

Spencer opened his mouth and started to smile. Midway, it collapsed to a frown. "No."

"Think harder," Jade said, feeling her heart beginning to pound. Maybe Christmas miracles were possible. Maybe Sylvia Bloomfield had come to her senses, remembered her duty to her office, her wedding vows to her husband and finally gotten rid of her boyfriend. Maybe she was calling to offer her an apology and her job back. "Maybe it wasn't a man."

"It was a woman."

Her body trembled with the force of new possibilities. "Sylvia Bloomfield?"

"Her office, but some other lady. Corinne something."

She frowned. Why would Corinne Palmer be calling? Sylvia wouldn't involve anyone else in such a sensitive situation. Unless Sylvia was too embarrassed to make the call herself.

"What time did she call?" she asked, looking at her watch.

"Around seven."

"Seven a.m.? Spencer, that was almost four hours ago."

He reached over to give her shoulder a comforting squeeze. "Calm down, kiddo. It's probably nothing important."

"How would you know?" Jade asked, twisting around to make certain the phone was still in the same place it had been for the last fourteen years.

"She said something about needing to talk to you about redecorating your office."

"Redecorating my office? Really?" Jade pressed her hands against her breastbone as the implication began sinking in. So her suspicion was true. Sylvia had come to her senses. Jade grabbed Spencer's biceps and gave him a shake. "That's great. Wonderful. Terrific!" Wrapping her arms around him, she threw herself into a hearty hug.

"It is?"

"Yes. Aren't you listening?" she asked, looking up at him before giving him an extra squeeze. She dropped her cheek against the hollow of his shoulder and sighed with happiness. "I'm having my office redone!"

Her spontaneous embrace soon became an exquisite entwining of two still bodies. The sensation of his body snug against her own answered questions she'd wondered about. And raised a few she hadn't. Then Spencer glided his hands to the small of her back and she held her breath. The delicate pressure molded more of her body to his as he brushed his lips against her ear in a delicate kiss.

Or was it a kiss?

"Congratulations, boss lady. But just what did you have to do for it?"

Four

Heck, no, it wasn't a kiss.

Jade pulled back within the circle of his arms, now banded around her as securely as straps of steel. "What did I have to do for it?" Bracing her hands against his rock-hard biceps, she stared into his steady blue gaze. "What kind of a crack is that?"

"Bloomfield suddenly sends word on Christmas Eve that she's having your office redecorated?" He made a clicking sound with his tongue then shook his head. "We're talking heavy-duty, very-merry gratitude here."

As he slid his hands around to her hips, a tingle of alarm started up her spine. "Can you be just a bit more obtuse?" she asked, hoping her knitted brows would take his attention away from her trembling. She hadn't felt this close to being found out since that panic attack on the train.

"Sure," he said, his innocent tone a welcome sound to her still tickly ear. "Whatever happened to onyx pen sets and fruit baskets?"

She forced a dry laugh from high in her throat, and prayed silently that it had sounded genuine. "Spencer, having my office redecorated isn't a Christmas gift from my boss."

"Really?" He pushed out his lower lip and squinted with confusion. Or was that doubt? She squinted back. Which one was it?

She tried keeping her focus on his eyes, but the rich, sweet scent of caffe latte clinging to his lips proved to be too distracting. Her gaze drifted to the moist sheen there. Divinely distracting. Everything about him was distracting.

Spencer lowered his head closer, then tilted it to one side. "Are you sure?"

"It's true...I swear," Jade murmured as she felt herself slipping into his spell again. Her eyes were already closing as she raised up on tiptoe.

"Then what job-well-done is it for, Jade?"

She blinked twice before coming to her senses and dropping back on her heels. "If that was supposed to be funny, it wasn't," she said, shoving her hands hard against his chest.

He released her instantly, giving her the space she sought but taking her balance in the process. As she began reeling backward, his lightning-quick reflexes kicked in. Catching her hand, he pulled her back. They slammed together, cheek to cheek, hip to hip and every inch in between. She clung to him for several thumping heartbeats as she imagined the two of them in the same tight and provocative embrace, only horizontal this time.

"Hey, boss lady," he said, his baritone voice muffling in her tousled hair, "I didn't know you could tango. Maybe you could give me a few lessons."

"That isn't funny, either," she said, her voice raspier this time as she began easing slowly and, as much as she hated to admit it, reluctantly, out of his embrace. It wasn't funny; it was the sexiest thing that ever happened to her. And he had to go and blow it by calling her boss lady.

Stepping back, she brushed at her bangs and silently swore she was going to make another appointment with that therapist and keep it this time. "Not that it's any of your business, Mr. Inquiring-Minds-Want-To-Know, but the office has needed redoing since the Ford administration. The carpet is threadbare, the draperies are dry-rotted and...and the chairs don't match."

He nodded slowly, as if he were waiting to hear more.

That warning tingle was back. This time beneath her rib cage. Shifting her weight from one foot to the other, she rubbed at her forehead then scratched at the side of her mouth. Spencer couldn't possibly know that this surprise redecorating was Sylvia's way of offering the proverbial olive branch, albeit, a gold-plated one.

Crossing her arms, she tucked her shaking hands behind them. The smartest thing she could do would be to keep her mouth shut and allow Spencer to speak, but waiting for him to respond was making her lips itch. "I...I mean, this is the perfect time to have it done." She pressed her hand against her red cashmere sweater. "I'll be out of the office for a couple of weeks. We've been on a list, you see, and I guess we were pushed a-h-head...."

His gaze continued boring into hers with the probing strength of two bright blue searchlights. She gave a short, impatient sigh and threw up her hands. "Spencer, what do you care that my office is being redone?"

As the corners of his eyes began to crinkle, two deep dimples appeared through his beard stubble to bracket his mouth. Suddenly his white teeth flashed. "I don't. I was trying to figure out if you subscribe to the trickle-down theory."

"Of economics?"

"Of gratitude. And how that might affect me, your personal assistant, come Christmas morning."

Before she could respond, he held up his hand.

"Please," he said, backing away with a comically humble bow. "Surprise me."

Jade watched as Spencer grabbed his jacket from the hook, waved goodbye to Megan and left the café. She was nibbling the inside of her cheek as he walked past the window with the stenciled reindeer. Not that she'd ever admit it, but even with his unnerving stares and questionable comments, there was something about Spencer Madison that tickled more than her ear.

Shaking her head, she laughed softly to herself before reaching for the wall phone and placing the return call to Washington. While she waited for her call to be answered, she pictured her and Spencer at the reunion. Now that she was about to receive official word that she had her job back, she could afford to relax. Laugh a little. Maybe buy him something fun for Christmas. Maybe even dance with him at the reunion. But not a tango. It would have to be a slow dance, because she could never imagine engaging in those precise and provocative moves without feeling like she was making a spectacle of herself. She closed her eyes as the phone on the other end continued ringing.

Spencer would have to hold her again, and this time she wouldn't push him away when his lips touched her ear. She imagined him laughing, teasing, whispering…dancing closer and closer…his hard thighs brushing against hers as they moved around the old gymnasium floor. She smoothed a hand over her hip where his had rested minutes before. The steady weight and gentle pressure of her own touch were poor alternatives for the way Spencer's body had felt against hers.

Her fingertips began straying over the top of her thigh. The soft, scratchy wool of her slacks sent tickling sparks spiraling up into the intimate recesses of her body. Maybe she wouldn't insist he shave off that sexy beard stubble after all.

"Representative Bloomfield's office."

Jade's eyelids fluttered opened. Jerking her hand from her thigh, she pushed off the wall as if the wallpaper had suddenly caught fire.

"Corinne?" Jade slapped her hand around the receiver. "Corinne, I'm sorry I didn't get back to you sooner, but I just got the message that you called." She slid one hand from the bottom of the receiver to grasp the metal-encased phone cord. "What's up?" she asked, as anticipation sent her heart rate soaring.

"Sylvia asked me to meet her here in the office yesterday afternoon. She wanted to finish up on some last-minute correspondence before she flew off for the holidays." Corinne gave a nervous laugh. "You know Sylvia. Before I knew what was happening, I had this redecorating project dropped in my lap. You should have heard her. 'Out with the old and in with the new, as soon as possible, Corinne.'"

Jade pictured Sylvia coming to her senses, calling up her driver and speeding to the Capitol Hill office to perform this act of penance. After being fired during an emotional three-way exchange over locked versus closed office doors, the vision of a humbled Sylvia warmed her. "It's Christmas Eve morning. I hope she didn't insist you spend your holiday in the office on my account."

"She didn't. I hadn't any plans to leave town. And to tell you the truth, I couldn't wait to get the ball rolling on this redecorating. What do you think of navy blue and cream?"

"Throw in some burgundy accents and it's my idea of heaven."

"I like it. I like it," Corinne said with a little girl giddiness that sent Jade into a fit of silly laughter.

"Jade, you sound so upbeat. I guess you won't mind if I read this letter to you that she had me type up."

The first niggling suspicion that something was wrong started over her scalp in a slow crawl. "What letter?"

"I'll just read it. It's not very long." Paper rattled as Corinne cleared her throat. 'To whom it may concern. Jade Macleod has been in my employ for three years. She has performed her duties in the areas of legislative research in an adequate manner during this time. Sincerely.' Etcetera, etcetera.

"Isn't that just like Sylvia to write something like that, Jade?"

Jade could only stare through a sprinkling of black stars at the stranglehold she had on the phone cord. After a few seconds she rubbed her eyes, but the stars stubbornly refused to leave her field of vision. Not only was she still without a job, she was now without a decent reference letter to secure another one. The reference letter she'd been pinning her future career hopes on. "Just like her," she managed to murmur.

"So, let's have it. What fabulous job did you land that made Sylvia mad enough to write this sorry excuse of a recommendation letter?"

"What job?" Jade repeated tonelessly.

"Not telling? That's okay if you want to keep quiet about it awhile longer. This way I'll sound as surprised as everyone else when we find out. And since Sylvia promoted me from administrative assistant to your old position, I have a ton of files to go through. By the way, I'm sending you the letter I just read to you along with a few other things you left behind. There wasn't much. Just a few computer disks and the onyx pen set Sylvia gave you."

That damn onyx pen set—the very thing Spencer had mentioned as an appropriate gift from her boss! Jade had treasured the pen set, given to her by Sylvia when she respected and admired the woman. Those sentiments had been instantly and drastically altered the moment she'd walked in on Sylvia and Lance. She winced as the scene played through her mind like an X-rated movie. Less than an hour later, Jade had packed up her personal belongings, heading for the door and purposely leaving the engraved pen set behind.

Now, like a bad penny, the damned thing was coming back to her along with a letter that wasn't worth the paper it was printed on, much less the time it took to read it, tear it up and stomp on it. She shook her head at the irony. "Thank you, Corinne. Good luck with the new job."

"Good luck with yours, and Merry Christmas."

Jade replaced the receiver then dropped her backside against the wall. "Merry Christmas? I don't think so," she whispered, staring straight ahead to nowhere. It took all her effort not to slide down to the floor onto her haunches and cry.

When Dickens's *A Christmas Carol* sprang to mind, she began wallowing in gloomy images from the tragic tale. But not for long. One-person pity parties were not her style. Besides, she was far from being cold or homeless or without loved ones.

She thought about her family and friends at last night's party. No one could ask for a more loving, more supportive group of people. She drummed her fingers against the wall. And how had she shown her gratitude since she'd been back in Follett River?

By avoiding their questions. By straight-out lying. And by bringing a stranger into their midst. A stranger named Spencer Madison who had her feeling up her own leg.

She pressed her hands to her face and gave into the groan she'd been careful to suppress during her conversation with Corinne. There would be no more fantasizing about Spencer's kisses or caresses. And cuddling up to him for a dance at the reunion was definitely out.

Her few relationships with men had never been of a-day-at-the-beach variety. So she had no business wondering what it would be like to take a dip in that deep ocean of testosterone marked Spencer Madison. Besides, she had more important things to do. Like networking with her associates. Like polishing her résumé. Like deciding where she could send it without that worthless, if not downright damaging, letter of recommendation Corinne had just read to her.

In the meantime, she wasn't ruining anyone's holiday by announcing she'd been fired then sent on her way with nothing more than an onyx pen set and that letter. Her face stung at the thought of it. If she kept on thinking about it, she'd be reduced to tears in a matter of seconds.

Jade gave in to a rough sigh as she attempted to pull herself together. This was not the end of her life. She was worth more than that letter. She was an intelligent woman with great work experience. She would figure a way out of the mess she was in. But first she had to get control of her emotions.

"Deep breath, Jade, and focus on the positive," she whispered to herself. "You can do this." She drew tight circles at her temples. "You will succeed because you're in control. And you're in control because you know you did nothing to be ashamed of."

"Hey, boss lady."

Jade fingers stiffened at her temples. She raised her eyes. A grinning Spencer stood before her with a paper bag in one hand and a small blue box in the other.

"Did I get the right kind?" he asked.

"Oh, God. What control?" she whispered before dragging a curtain of red-gold curls over her eyes.

Jade's euphoric mood of fifteen minutes ago had vanished into the biggest blue funk Spence had ever seen. He didn't have to ask. He knew from that strange pinging sensation in his gut that her return call to Washington hadn't turned out the way she expected. Spencer dropped the box of tampons back into the bag then stared at Jade for a full five seconds before setting it on a chair.

His first inclination was to put his arms around her and tell her that whatever the problem was he'd help her fix it. He reached in her direction but stopped his hand in midair. Where the hell was his brain? Did he honestly want to tangle himself up in her troubles? Not likely! He'd already come close to committing career suicide once. He had no desire to make that mistake again.

Bringing his hand back, he raked his fingers through his hair. Besides, if his original suspicion that Jade was involved in Bloomfield's travel-fraud schemes were true, he didn't need personal matters complicating his work, or calling it into question later on by the editor of *Independence* magazine.

So why was he still looking at her as if the possibility existed that he could have her? Why was he still wasting his time wondering how it would feel to remove her barrette and sink his fingers in that soft, gold-shot cloud of red hair that she kept plastered back most of the time? Why was he still thinking about how her mouth would taste on his? Why was he still imagining the soft, feminine sounds she would make when he told her what he was thinking about in bed this morning around two? And then again around five.

Spencer ran his knuckles over his Adam's apple as he tried and failed to pull his gaze away from Jade. If he *could* start down the road to romance with this beautiful, intelligent, vulnerable, maddening woman, he could easily envision himself not wanting to turn back.

He sighed roughly and lowered his hand. Dumb ''if'', he thought, because no amount of soft, gooey sentiment could ever change the truth Jade would eventually have to hear. Without her insider input to strengthen his exposé, he might as well forget about being offered a permanent position at *Independence* magazine.

He was not caving in to a little tingle in his blood and a slight tug in his groin—okay, a big tug in his groin. Flexing his hands, he shoved them in his pockets. He'd waited too long for this career opportunity. No way was he staying in tabloid hell writing "The Mad Man" a day more than he had to. Besides, another cold shower tonight wouldn't kill him.

"Bad news from the front?"

Jade's head came up slowly, her eyes shimmering with indecision. Behind them the cappuccino machine softly gurgled and whooshed. "And if there were?"

She'd never looked more desirable, or more desiring than she did at that moment. "You need to talk to someone? I'm your man." He fought off the urge to wince. *I'm your man?* Listen to yourself, Spence, ol' boy. Wrong words!

A soft, pained smile began to curve her lips. "Are you?" she whispered.

His heart knocked a warning message in his chest, but he ignored it. "You bet," he said, suddenly craving the woman he'd just forbidden himself from having. He knew he had no right to respond to this pull he felt toward her, but second by second he felt his resolve slipping. "Jade," he whispered softly.

Moistening her lips, she took a step forward.

He started to pull his hands from his pockets.

She opened her mouth to speak, and a cup and spoon crashed to the floor a few feet away. Someone swore and the fragile connection they'd forged shattered as surely as the small white cup.

"There's no big crisis," Jade said, in tones crisp enough for a drill sergeant. She reached around him to take her purse from the chair. "Just a disagreement on a color scheme." She slung the leather strap over her shoulder then adjusted the fit of her watch. "But there's not going to be that kind of problem picking out a suit for you. Is there?"

He shrugged, as if the tender moment they'd just been through hadn't happened. "Shouldn't be."

They argued the whole time they shopped, but in the end he gave in and agreed that the navy blue suit would do. Choosing a tie was another matter. She wanted the one with the paisley pattern in blue, cream and burgundy. He didn't want a tie. He wanted a banded collar shirt. They finally agreed to buy both and decide later on what he would wear to the reunion dinner dance.

While the harmless squabbling appeared to take her mind off her troubles and the edge off her tension, he knew Jade was far from calm since that telephone call. And that confused him more than ever about her travel-fraud involvement. The few times he casually asked about her job-related traveling, she was eager to tell him in detail about the work she'd accomplished.

Had she been traveling with Sylvia Bloomfield at the taxpayers' expense for lavish stays at posh resorts or had Jade been working her fanny off on legitimate fact-finding trips as she had told him? Was it possible that Jade had been covering up for Sylvia's misuse of taxpayers' money? Or had Sylvia managed not to involve Jade in any of it? And how did any of those possibilities connect with Jade being fired?

Sitting beside the Macleod family Christmas tree the next morning, Spence was still uncertain about everything. Except for one thing.

While Jade was doing an admirable job at appearing relaxed, he knew she was nearing the breaking point again. He'd seen the light under the door and heard her walking around her room at three o'clock this morning. When he'd called through the door to ask if she was all right, his only answer had been a click of her light switch and the dark silence that had followed.

Looking at her now with those faint smudges of tired violet beneath her eyes, he came to a decision. If only for a day or two, he was going to do everything he could to keep her mind off of her career problems. He wanted to believe his reason for lightening her load had to do with Christmas, goodwill and pure compassion for her rattled state. But that wasn't his only aim.

Sooner or later, human nature being what it was, Jade was going to have to talk to someone about the mess her life was in. Since she continued to play the role of a happy and successful professional with her family and friends, spilling her guts to them appeared more and more unlikely. On the other hand, she'd come close to opening up to him on several occasions. Optimizing the chance that she would choose him to listen became his new obsession.

He knew the first thing she needed was downtime from her troubles. He'd already planned a good dose of Christmas, complete with armloads of presents, a generous amount of laughter, a touch of teasing and whatever else he could think of to make her see him as her trusted ally. In a few days, when the pressures of her situation started again, she would feel the need more than ever to talk. When that time came—and it would—he would be her man. All friendly smiles. All ears. All ready to work her words into his exposé and his way into a new job.

Five

_____

Spence bit off a chunk of Christmas cookie and chewed it slowly as he looked across the living room at Jade. She sat on the arm of her mother's chair, her head bent in purposeful concentration as she twisted a new silk scarf, his gift to Mrs. Macleod, into a loose rope. Morning sunlight streaming through the window was making Jade's red-gold hair shimmer and her fair skin glow. How any man could leave her was beyond his comprehension. He swallowed his mouthful of toasted almond shortbread then lowered his hand to his bent knee. If he were her man...*her man?*

The words turned on him like a rebounding arrow from Cupid's bow. And like a warrior at the brink of battle, he forced himself to look her way again as he steeled himself against the onslaught of tender emotions.

"Let's try it this way," Jade said, gently looping the colorful silk around her mother's neck.

"That looks so beautiful, dear," Mrs. Macleod said, as she twisted in her chair to look into a gilt-framed wall mirror. Smiling at her reflection, the older woman caught Spencer's eye as she patted her daughter's hand. "In shades of teal. Spencer. How did you know teal is my favorite color?"

"Because he asked me, Mother," Jade said as she shot Spence a look of gentle reprimand.

"I see," Mrs. Macleod said, her bright eyes practically twinkling with delight. "How wonderful that the both of you worked together on my present." Reaching to slip on her reading glasses she flipped up the scarf tail for a detailed inspection of the hand-rolled hem. "It's just the loveliest thing. I'm going to wear it at our New Year's Eve brunch."

As the older woman continued praising the gift to her husband and son, Jade walked back to Spencer and took the space next to him on the floor beside the tree.

"I saw that scarf at Mr. Jordan's yesterday," she said in a conspiratorial whisper. "It cost a small fortune."

But aren't you the one, Jade, who loves showy displays of gratitude? he wanted to ask. Instead, he smiled then reached out to gently squeeze her shoulder. "The price of the scarf was nothing compared to your family's generosity. They brought the spirit of the season alive by giving this stranger a place to stay."

Tears began glistening in her eyes and he wondered if he'd gone too far. He hadn't lied about his feelings for her family, but he knew before he spoke that this morning was already difficult enough for her. Surrounded by her loving family, she must have been thinking about her continuing dishonesty with them.

"They've always..." She stopped to swallow back tears. "You know, they've always been here for me. It's so good to be able to trust the people you love. Isn't it?"

Spencer managed a guilty nod.

"Hey, sis," Neal said, breaking into a moment Spencer was going to remember all of his life. "Aren't you going to give Spence his gifts?"

"Yes," she said, shifting her gaze to stare at her brother. "I guess Santa didn't deliver that box of patience I requested in your name."

As she tried to tug a heavy package from beneath the branches of the twelve-foot tree, Spence shoved the rest of the cookie into his mouth and reached in to help her. Together they dragged the box out from under the tree and between them.

Looking from her to the box then back to her again, he raised his brows. "I can't imagine what this is," he said, sliding his gaze toward the Macleod family. "Any guesses?"

Jade squirmed uncomfortably as the Macleods strained for a better look. Her mother smiled, her brother shrugged and her father just shook his head.

"Whatever it is, she's sure to surprise you," Mr. Macleod said.

"Just open it," Jade said as she rolled her gaze toward the Christmas tree.

Spence shoved his thumbs into two folds and neatly peeled the red foil down one side of the box. When he saw what she'd given him, he let out a theatrical gasp of surprise. "Ahh, boss lady, you shouldn't have."

Mr. Macleod leaned forward in his armchair as his wife raised her camera and snapped a photo. "What have you got there?"

"Computer paper, sir. Five thousand sheets."

"Computer paper?" Neal asked before howling with laughter. Jade's face colored to match the red foil wrapping paper Spencer was still holding.

"There's more," she said, reaching under the tree again then shoving a second package one foot across the polished floor at the edge of the Oriental rug.

"I would hope so, darling," her mother said in an unmistakably disappointed voice.

Dropping the wrapping paper, Spencer picked up the second package, held it to his ear and shook it. Smiling, he peeled back the wrapping paper. "Just what I needed," he announced, giving her a wink as he held up a dictionary for her family to see. "Words to put on my new paper."

"A dictionary?" her family asked in varying tones of disbelief and disappointment.

The beautiful redhead kneeling beside him eased her bottom back on her ankles. "Honestly, we're all too old for this," she said, as she snatched the red foil paper from Spence and crushed it between her hands. "It isn't as if anyone here still believes in Santa Claus."

"But we will once we have grandchildren," Mrs. Macleod said to Spence.

As Jade said a frantic and not too quiet prayer, Mr.

Macleod ran his thumb along the new pipe Spencer had given him. "Jade's always been a practical girl."

"I'll say," Neal said. "Remember that pint-size vacuum cleaner she gave me when I was twelve? And her hand-drawn cartoon on how to clean my room with it?"

While the Macleods began reciting other practical gifts Jade had given them over the years, Spencer gave Jade a teasing, closemouthed smile.

"Do I get any instructions with my gifts?" he whispered, wishing he could give her the hug he wanted to give, the hug he knew she needed.

"Not really," she said, picking a piece of glittery tinsel from the knee of her white wool slacks. She wound the strand of silver around her index finger as her expression became serious again. "Just a suggestion that you spend more time in your room working on your book," she said quietly.

She started to get up, but he took her hand and held her down.

"I'll keep that in mind, boss lady. Meanwhile, this is for you," he said, settling a box in her lap. "From me. If you need any instructions or assistance with it...well, that's what I'm here for."

As if on cue, Jade's family stopped talking and turned their attention toward her. She looked at them and then back at Spencer. "What is it?" she asked suspiciously.

He smiled and nodded for her to open it. "Something practical."

She gave him a warning look, then cautiously peeled back the paper and opened the lid.

"Oh," she said, breathing a highly noticeable sigh

of relief. "Relaxation tapes. This was very thoughtful. I mean it."

"There's more," Spencer said, enjoying her smile much more than he had a right to. When she tucked her hair behind one ear, the palms of his hands itched to do it, too. For once she'd foregone the tightly secured hairstyle she usually wore for a shoulder tickling, free-for-all halo of red-gold curls and waves.

She set aside the shrink-wrapped four-pack of tapes then reached into the soft nest of tissue paper. "And a candle." Her warning look had softened to a cautious one when she lifted the thick wax cylinder to her nose. "A chocolate-scented candle," she said in an amazed tone before breaking up into laughter. "Where did you find this?"

"It's white chocolate and I always guard my source," he said, as he pointed back to the box again. "One more."

"Spencer," she said, a teasing reprimand evident in the way she dragged out the last syllable.

He saw a glimpse of the little girl in her and thanked a higher power for the privilege. Shaking her head, she pulled out a pretty glass jar then silently read the label. Her eyes widened momentarily.

"What is it, darling?" her mother asked.

"It's just bubble bath, Mom," she said, then quickly returned the jar to the bottom of the box.

"Scented bubble bath, Mrs. Macleod," Spence said. "It's part of an aromatherapy line designed to reduce stress." He turned back to Jade and gave her a private smile. "She's been working very hard, Mrs. Macleod."

"Thank you, Spencer," Jade said, in a clipped tone

that made it clear he'd said enough. She fidgeted restlessly as her gaze darted back and forth between him and the gift box. Suddenly that big, blue-eyed gaze locked onto his.

"That's what I'm here for. To make your job a little easier," he said, sensing a new kind of energy building between them. That one-of-a-kind energy that superseded his fascination with her little-girl look of wonder he'd been enjoying a moment before.

"Isn't that adorable?" Mrs. Macleod asked.

Jade dropped her forehead against her raised hand and gave a loud sigh. "Isn't what adorable?"

"That you two gave each other gifts to make your work a little easier. Honestly, it's just amazing how much the two of you have in common. I was just saying to your father—"

"Mother," she said, shoving the lid on the box as she stood, "I know what you're up to and I'm not going to let you get away with it."

"Whatever are you talking about, dear?" Mrs. Macleod asked as Jade began crossing the room toward the double doors.

Spencer stood and followed close behind her. When Jade suddenly stopped, his hands shot forward, closing around her arms in a move to steady her.

"You're trying to make us a couple. We are not a couple. We are simply two people working together," she said, looking back over her shoulder at him. "Isn't that right, Spencer?"

"Absolutely," he said as Jade's mother snapped their photo. "I couldn't imagine thinking of you in any other way." He glanced at the Macleods then back to her. "It's unthinkable. Just the idea of you and me, two co-workers, engaged in anything—"

Jade glowered a warning at him as she stepped away. "I think they get the idea." Shifting the box to her hip, she turned and walked out into the foyer.

"But where are you going?" Mrs. Macleod called after them.

"Must have something to do with that secret project they're working on, Mom," Neal said in a devilishly loud voice.

Spence gave a thumbs-up to Neal before following Jade out of the room and across to the curving staircase. "Seriously, you're not my type."

"Okay," she said, slamming a hand on the banister as she turned to face him. "I get the picture."

She headed on up the stairs, her red-gold hair shimmering and bouncing near her shoulders like a halo of tantalizing flames. Spence shook his head with admiration as he took in the sight before him. She had more going for her than a good hair day. Her curvy hips and long, slender legs were a dream come true. Or, in his case, only a part of a dream that had yet to come true. He shook his head in disbelief at the crazy possibilities he was entertaining. He had to get a major grip. This sexual-attraction thing was too damn close to the reason he'd given up his career as a foreign correspondent. The memories made him wince.

"Look, Jade," he said in a serious tone, "even if you were my type, an affair in the workplace is never a smart move. People are asking for problems when they allow that sort of thing to happen," he said, increasing his speed to keep up with her.

She didn't turn around, but kept on going. Because

of that, he didn't know if she was listening to what he was saying, but *he* damn sure was. His goal was to get his story, and allowing anything else to interfere was asking for trouble. *Anything* else, like Jade's backside moving in that tantalizing rhythm a few feet above and ahead of him on the stairs.

"Once you start making eyes at someone, it's only a matter of time before things get out of hand and you're getting caught between the file cabinets. Then it's—" He broke off when she suddenly stopped and turned.

"But we *don't* work together." She looked back at the open double doors to the living room and rolled her eyes. Leaning down, she lowered her voice to a fierce whisper. "I would never have an office affair with you, even if we did work together. And what's more, you're not *my* type. So I most certainly could not imagine us making love on top of a desk."

His arms splayed wide by his sides. "Who said anything about making love on top of a desk?"

"You just did." She leaned closer to him. "You said—" The unfinished sentence hung in the air as her flushed face deepened to scarlet. The gift box shifted in her arm and the candle rolled out over the edge. They both reached for it, their cheeks bumping each other's as their fingers tangled around the thick white cylinder of wax. For another long moment neither of them said a word, made a sound or took a breath. Then she moved her face away from his.

Spencer didn't bother correcting her. They both knew she'd realized her mistake and was paying dearly for it. And besides that, he was too busy watching her perfectly pouty lips parting in shock. Or was it from something else? That one-of-a-kind something that both of them had been fighting. The moment pulsated with possibilities as the questions in her eyes continued to multiply. Questions he wanted to answer if he just knew what they were.

"Jade?" As he slid his hand around her waist, a glimmer of panic sharpened her soft expression. He would have backed off but there was an unmistakable shimmer of excitement there, too.

He pulled her closer as he repeated her name, in a whisper this time. A tiny sound broke in her throat a moment before she pressed her lips to his. He barely had time to register the sizzling moment in his consciousness before she pulled away, tugged the candle from his grasp and shoved it into the box.

"And—and as for that Tango Mango bubble bath…" she said, frantically struggling to fit the lid back on the box.

"Mango Tango," he corrected over the sound of rustling tissue paper and her thunking the lid against the box.

He gently lifted a few red hairs away from the side of her mouth and placed them behind her ear. His gesture caused her to freeze and her eyes to close in slow motion. When she opened them to his, their blue depths were filled with a myriad of messages. Curiosity, wonder, fear. Desire. Unmistakable, aching desire. He felt it, too. He whispered her name again, but more urgently this time as he drew a circle on her cheek with his thumb. "I didn't mean all that other stuff the way it sounded."

"Yes, you did," she said, trying with all her might to sound unaffected by the kiss and his tenderness.

"Jade, I swear—"

"Oh, please," she begged, unable to meet his eyes, "don't embarrass us by pretending you can take it back." Without another word, she hugged the box to her chest and fled up the stairs.

Spence leaned against the curved wall and watched her until she'd disappeared into her room. He stared at her door for several unsettling seconds then roughly drew his hand over his face.

He wasn't quite certain how he allowed it to happen but his goal of giving Jade downtime from her troubles had not been attained. "That's putting it mildly," he said to himself. Without thinking about the way he could be adding to her problems, he'd rushed headlong toward the lady, and in the process had scared her badly enough to send her running. He ran the moment through his mind again then scratched his head.

Or could someone else have put that look of fear and distrust in her big baby blues? He made a face. "Ah, yes...Richard," he said softly to himself. "Can't forget about him."

Spence shifted his backside against the wall as he thought about Jade's ex-boyfriend. Maybe Jade was telling the truth when she said Richard had devastated her by dumping her at the worst possible time. Had that jerk also managed to leave her suspicious of all other men, too?

As he thought about what he'd like to do to the bastard, another idea began crowding out the thought. He felt his forehead wrinkling with dismay. Was it possible that, when it came to men, she'd never *had* any confidence to begin with? He started to laugh at the thought, but checked himself. If that were the case, it would go far in explaining those curious looks she'd given him. Him? Could she honestly be looking at him to tap into that well of womanly sensuality and set her free?

Why not? She'd just kissed him. Well, technically it was more of a beginning to a kiss than a kiss, but who knew where it could go from there? Suddenly a rush of erotic images filled his mind, and more than ever, he wanted to... Wanted to what, dammit? Play Prince Charming to Sleeping Beauty and blow the best chance he'd had in years to reestablish his reputation as a journalist?

Spence pushed off the wall as he bit off a sharp, sibilant curse. While he was stroking his male ego with a lot of cocky, unsubstantiated gibberish, his career clock was ticking. He climbed the rest of the stairs and headed down the hall that led to his door. And past hers.

However much he ached to do it, he was not there to spend precious time unraveling the mystery of Jade's lack of womanly self-esteem, if there even was such a thing. He was there for a story, he reminded himself as his steps slowed to a stop in front of her door.

What he didn't want or need was anything complicating his chances of getting it. Anything such as embarrassing and alienating her more than he already had by asking her to explain that remark she'd made about making love on a desktop. Or trying to convince her that she was the sexiest, most intriguing female he'd ever met. Or suggesting that sometime in the future she might want to consider making love with him until the bed caught fire.

His shoulders sagged as he dropped his chin to his chest. What he had to do was stop this schizoid, testosterone-induced flip-flopping and focus on his goal. He also had to apologize to her for his behavior and tell her how much her friendship meant to him. That would work because it wasn't a total lie. Better than that, it might get them through the next week and a half without any more close encounters of the sexual kind.

He raised his fist to knock on her door, but picturing her on the other side, he slowly lowered his hand. She was probably still attempting to regain her composure. He imagined her sitting on the love seat…alone…facing the balcony that spanned both their bedrooms…those soft, red gold curls framing that beautiful face…and those big blue eyes asking, "Why?"…while her full, peaked breasts, sleek, curvy hips and waiting embrace answered, "Why not?"

Suddenly that tug in his groin was back, big-time. He stepped away from the door; he could talk to her later. Meanwhile, he could probably fit in another cold shower before lunch.

Since that prickly-tickly, bump-and-go kiss on the stairs, Jade had made it a point to steer clear of Spencer as often as possible. She spent half the day after Christmas in her room working on her résumé and the other half helping her mother with plans for the New Year's Eve brunch. When members of her high school French club invited her to an impromptu luncheon the next day, she left the house early and came back late. As luck would have it, she needn't have worried about working side by side with Spencer while they decorated the gym for the reunion. Neal kept him busy that morning with an amateur basketball tournament before dropping him off at the gym…just as she was leaving it. She arrived home in time to take the package that Corinne had promised to, and did, send, from the delivery man. Then she promptly threw it in the back of her closet, unopened.

Her luck, dubious as it might be, was still holding when Neal announced that he and Casey were working on a second installment to the story of her visit. Envisioning the ten minutes alone in the car with Spencer on the way to the high school that night, Jade quickly asked for her and Spencer to ride along with them.

Her luck ran out the moment Neal and Casey finished hanging up their coats. "See you later, sis," he said, hurrying into the gym with Casey and her camera at his side.

"Neal, wait up," she said, slamming her evening bag on a table.

"You can catch him later," Spencer said calmly as he helped her off with her coat and hung it up. "In the meantime, I've been waiting for the right moment to—"

"Well, this isn't the right moment," she said, turning away from Spencer to adjust the jeweled comb that was already tucked tightly into her neat French twist.

She thought back to the scene in her house twenty minutes earlier. Trying to convince her mother that this wasn't exactly prom night only prolonged the ordeal of posing for pictures on the staircase with him. Being forced to stare at him once tonight was more than enough and this time her mother wasn't around to insist.

Spence moved in front of her, blocking her view of the gym.

"Was it the right moment when you kissed me?"

Her gaze lifted and locked on him.

He'd shaved off his beard stubble without being reminded, slapped on aftershave that should have come with a warning and worn that white silk, banded collar shirt that added the perfect amount of panache to an already sensational look. She tried to swallow and almost choked. He was beyond sensational. She closed her eyes as wild words strung together in her mind. Touchable ... delicious ... achy ... needy ... not later ... now ... right now ... show me how ... how much ...

"That was *not* a kiss! That was an accident," she said, letting go of her hair and the comb to make her point with a sweep of her hands. The comb slipped and her hair dropped over the nape of her neck. Grabbing for the ornament, she only succeeded in snarling hair around it.

"Here. Let me help," he said, guiding her to a shadowy corner then moving in close enough for her to feel his breath on her forehead. While she kept her gaze trained on his lapel and her hands flat against her midriff, he carefully unwound several curly strands from the amber-toothed comb.

"You ought to wear your hair down more often." Fluffing it around her face, he touched the comb to the sides. "Like this."

"You're doing it again," she said, taking back the comb.

"Doing what?"

Making me wonder what it's like to have you look at me and touch me and get this close...and even closer while we're naked and alone. She shook her head. "Just forget I said I was dreading this reunion because Richard left me and I had no one to come with. You're not my date tonight. You don't have to hang around me and say things you don't mean."

He studied her for a long, uncomfortable moment as the sound of laughter and light music filtered into the anteroom. "Whether I hang around you or not, people are bound to ask me questions."

"What kind of questions?" she asked, wondering if he meant personal questions about them. She blew a soft stream of air up over her face. Lord, who knew a short, sleeveless, black velvet cocktail dress could be so hot?

"I don't know," he said, sliding his hands in his pockets and shrugging. "What do I do as your assistant? What's the private Sylvia Bloomfield like? Where is she spending the holidays?"

"Tell them you assist me with my research." She picked at the neckline of her dress as she began backing away toward the entrance to the gym. "Tell them Sylvia Bloomfield is a very busy woman. And she's spending the holidays in the Virgin Islands."

"Virgin Islands?" He caught her arm and moved her out of the way as two people walked by. "What's she doing down there? I heard a rumor she was joining her family at their ski lodge near Aspen."

"Did I say Virgin Islands?" she asked, as she pictured the travel brochures scattered on the rug in front of the desk where she'd discovered Sylvia and Lance. "Of course, she's spending the holiday skiing with her family. Look, I doubt anyone in Follett River cares who members of Congress are spending their holidays with."

"Who?"

"I meant where, and for security reasons we shouldn't even be talking about this."

"You look nervous, Jade. Is everything okay?"

Before she could answer, Megan walked into the anteroom.

"Hi, you two," she said, "Neal told me you'd arrived. I'm on my way to find a microphone, but I wanted to tell you both again how much I appreciated your help decorating today. Everyone's getting a real kick out of how we've recreated prom night, even down to those paper models of the Eiffel Tower." She laughed and shook her head. "It kind of feels like prom night, doesn't it, Jade? Except you can't be sure who will walk in," she said, looking at the row of outside doors across the hall.

Jade's hands were sweating; she was worrying about her hair and arguing with the guy who brought her. She picked up her evening bag from the table and slipped the comb inside. "It definitely feels like prom night."

"You ought to wear your hair down like that more often. And don't look so worried," Megan said as she moved across the anteroom and through a door marked Audio/Visual. "I'm sure your speech will be fine."

"Speech?" Jade grabbed for Spencer's hand and pulled him toward her. "What is she talking about?"

"Hey. Don't look at me. When I got back from hanging streamers today, I know I slipped one of those programs under your door," he said, pointing to a stack of papers on a nearby table. "Didn't you read it?"

"No, I did not," she said indignantly as she removed her hand from his. She took a program from the stack and scanned down until she saw her name. "I'm supposed to talk about the meaning of success." She whacked the paper against her thigh. "Spencer! Why didn't you say something?"

"Every time I tried, you told me it wasn't a good time to talk to you. Remember?"

She narrowed her eyes.

He leaned forward, and just as she thought he would kiss her, he moved his face to the side of hers. "Next time, Jade."

"Next time," she said, echoing his tone as a delicious shiver cascaded over body.

Moving back, he ran his index finger down her nose then across one cheekbone. "Next time will be the right time."

Jade watched him walk into the gym, his self-assurance evident in his squared shoulders and relaxed stride. Someone reached out a hand and Spence shook it. In a matter of seconds he disappeared into a group of men who were talking loudly and proudly about their racquetball scores.

It took her a few minutes before her knees stopped shaking and she could manage to put one foot in front of the other and march herself into the gym.

"These are my friends. I'm going to have a good time, too," she mumbled with enough uncertainty to add, "I really am."

For the next two hours she was torn between the surprisingly good time she was having and the crazy desire to share that news with Spencer. Few people tried to dig deeper than a polite question or two about the position they believed she still held on Capitol Hill. Although she sat at the same table with Spencer, she spent the time listening to the Thompson twins talk about their car-wash franchise, Jane Montague's third, bloodletting divorce and Parker McPhee's suggestions on where to invest the paycheck she was no longer receiving.

Through dinner and well into the dancing, she noticed Spencer wasn't lacking for conversation or companionship, either. Every time Jade caught a glimpse of him, he was not only adding to his fan club, it appeared he was turning it into his harem.

Crossing her arms tightly across her midriff, her subtle glances turned into outright staring. She tapped her fingernails against her evening bag as a former classmate shared a laugh and touched him on the arm. Jade shifted her weight from one high-heeled pump to the other. *Harem* was the right word for it, but if she asked Spencer, he'd probably tell her it was research for his novel. One of these days she was going to insist on a peek at his computer screen.

Jade glanced at her two friends standing next to her for momentary reassurance that she wasn't alone. Rebecca Barnett and Megan Sloan had seen her through the few problem times she'd had in high school, but those problems paled next to this new and confusing mess. She wondered what they thought about the sudden popularity of her assistant, but decided not to ask because of the questions that would follow. She looked back at Spencer. How had this man, this stranger who would be in her life for such a short time, managed to send her into such a ripping jag of juvenile jealousy?

"Jade Macleod," Rebecca Barnett said, taking a step closer, "you look positively sophisticated in black velvet. Of course, ten years ago you looked sophisticated in jeans and a sweater. Didn't she, Megan?"

"Jade looked sophisticated in gym clothes," Megan said.

"I do? I did?" Jade asked, running her hand along the waist of her cocktail dress. Her gaze flickered back and forth between Spencer and her two friends.

"Yes, and yes again, Jade," Rebecca said.

Sure, Jade thought, sophisticated in a businesslike, but not in a sexy way.

Rebecca laughed softly. "Your assistant can't keep his eyes off you, either. Every time you're not looking at him, like right now, he ends up staring at those crisscross straps across your back."

Jade took a speedy glance over her shoulder then, more confused than ever, turned back to Megan and Rebecca. Why hadn't she been aware that he'd be looking at her before her friends had to tell her?

And what was he looking for? Did he expect her to make a complete idiot of herself if someone asked about a man in her life?

"Has he been doing that for long?"

Megan leaned close to one ear and Rebecca leaned

close to the other. ''All night,'' they crooned in a whispery duet.

The three of them turned their gazes again toward Spencer. He chose that moment to look their way and give a grin and a big wave. Megan and Rebecca waved back.

''So, tell us, Jade, what's it like working with *him* and Congresswoman Bloomfield?'' Rebecca asked,

''Oh, you know Washington,'' she said, reaching to pat her French twist and touching thick wavy curls instead. Because she hadn't brought her hair spray and because the ladies' room was crowded, she decided to leave it down. She touched the sides as Spencer had done. ''Never a dull moment.''

That was true, but if she talked about Sylvia and Spence and work, she'd be adding to her growing list of lies, and this time, telling them to two old and dear friends. Plastering on a smile, she gathered her energy and turned it on her friends. ''Can you believe it? We're back where we all started from, Follett River High. Things never really change, do they?''

For the first time since Jade had known Rebecca, the gorgeous brunette looked alarmed. ''Of course things change. Everything changes,'' Rebecca said with enough passion to make Jade blink. ''Excuse me. I have to fix my hair.''

Megan gave Jade a mysterious smile as Rebecca cut a speedy path away from them and across the dance floor.

''What was that all about?'' Jade asked.

''Are you ready for this?''

Jade was ready for anything that would take her mind off Spencer. She fought the urge to look at him again. "I can handle it," she said, suddenly feeling as if she were back in high school passing notes during study hall.

Megan looped her arm through Jade's. "Remember during our senior year, how bad things got between her and Raleigh Hanlon?"

"Mr. Hanlon? Raleigh Hanlon, our history teacher?"

"Yes."

Jade shook her head and laughed. "That had to have been the longest and most impressive student/teacher war in American history. Those two were like nitro and glycerin together."

"That was then, but people do change." Megan bit back a smile.

Jade stared, dumbfounded at her friend.

"Jade, don't look so shocked. He's a history professor at the college now and she's an adult."

"Mr. Hanlon and Reb Barnett, our favorite bad girl who vowed never to take any prisoners? The girl voted Most Likely To Redo The Ceiling Of The Sistine Chapel With A Can Of Spray Paint?" She slowly pulled her arm from Megan's. "No-o-o-o. I don't believe it. They can't be...lovers."

"Why not? Love is love, no matter how long it takes to find it." Megan let her smiling gaze stray toward Spencer and then brought it back to Jade. "Some people refuse to accept the obvious, even when it's right under their nose."

Pointedly ignoring Megan's not-so-hidden message, Jade cocked her head and gave her friend a challenging stare. "Well, if what you say is true, where is Mr. Hanlon tonight?"

"That's the question I've put off asking Rebecca all evening."

"I don't know, Meggie. I just can't imagine a more unlikely twosome than Reb and Mr. Hanlon falling in love."

Megan gave Spencer a tiny wave. "Can't you?" she asked before leaving Jade standing in the middle of the gym staring at him.

Spencer stared back with a look hot and potent enough to make her skin tingle, her hands begin to shake and a fine film of perspiration to break out on her forehead. Her bra was suddenly constricting her breathing, her panties were tickling where they shouldn't and heat was pooling in every erogenous place on her body. If this kept on much longer, she was sure one of them—probably her—would say or do something to the other that could lead to death by embarrassment.

When someone placed a yearbook in his hand, Jade quickly headed for the opposite side of the gym. She stayed there for the next fifteen minutes hashing out her reaction to Reb and Raleigh Hanlon's affair while trying not to think about Spencer. Why was she finding it so hard to accept that her high school friend and a former high school teacher had, ten years after those facts, fallen in love? After all, Rebecca was a true rebel spirit who had never let conventional behavior or self-doubt stand in her way. And it wasn't as if Rebecca Barnett and Raleigh were strangers to each other—unlike her and Spencer. Except that Spencer wasn't a stranger anymore.

She brushed a wavy lock of hair from the side of her face and exhaled roughly. Didn't she have enough to worry about without overanalyzing the hell out of her reaction to someone else's love life? Shouldn't she have her mind on something more important such as coming up with something clever to say to her old high school friends in the next twenty minutes? Except for that crazy moment when she'd obviously misinterpreted his look as one of interest, Spencer appeared quite content spending his time with everyone but her tonight. And what was so wrong about that? Steering clear of her was exactly what she ordered him to do.

She reached into her purse, pulled out her hair comb then slapped them both on a table. He was probably doing research for that novel he was writing, she told herself as she began hastily fashioning a French twist. She tried jamming the comb in place, but too much hair escaped before she could tuck it securely. Groaning, she stuck the comb between her teeth and began again. And failed again. What was happening to her? She could usually do her hair in the dark. In a windstorm. With her hands in mittens. When she didn't have Spencer Madison around to make her insides quiver.

She felt a light tap on her shoulder. Turning, she found herself looking up into Spencer's face. His calm expression only made her more aware of her own frenzied state.

"They're playing our song."

She pulled the comb from her mouth. "We don't have a song," she whispered.

He took the comb from her hand and tossed it on the table beside her evening bag. "We do now," he said, drawing her onto the dance floor.

Slipping his arm around her back, he offered his hand. "Tonight, boss lady, I'm leading."

This was it. The moment she could laugh him off. Or sternly tell him she didn't think this was funny. But the longer she looked into his eyes, the longer she felt his hand so pleasantly firm against her back, the longer he stood there looking so right, the more she knew she'd have to agree with him. Tonight, for a little while, he would lead and she would follow.

As the lights in the old gymnasium grew even dimmer, and the saxophone blew its sultry, seductive invitation to move in close, she placed her hand in his. Tomorrow if he mentioned this moment, she'd pass it off as a reaction to a few mixed drinks and a little reminiscing. He was probably dancing with her out of a sense of duty.

"How's that book of yours coming?" she asked, trying her best not to dance too close to him. "Are you getting much use out of that dictionary? I always dog-ear mine and—"

"Relax," he whispered as he slid his hand lower over the velvet strips crisscrossing her back. His fingertips intermittently stroked her bare skin between the bands of velvet before coming to rest at the small of her back. His slow motion move brought her hips against the beginning of his arousal. "Just go with me."

She tilted her head back.

"I won't dance you off the edge of the earth, Jade."

"But—"

He eased his hips away from hers and smiled down at her.

PLAY "LUCKY 7" AND GET
FIVE FREE GIFTS!

HOW TO PLAY:

1. With a coin, carefully scratch off the silver box at the right. Then check the claim cha to see what we have for you—**FREE BOOKS** and a gift—**ALL YOURS! ALL FREE!**

2. Send back this card and you'll receive brand-new Silhouette Desire® novels. These books have a cover price of $3.50 each, but they are yours to keep absolutely free.

3. There's no catch. You're under no obligation to buy anything. We charge nothing— ZERO—for your first shipmen And you don't have to make any minimum number of purchases—not even one!

4. The fact is thousands of readers enjoy receiving books by mail from the Silhouette Reader Service™ months before they're available in stores. They like the convenience of home delivery and they love our discount prices!

5. We hope that after receiving your free books you'll want to remain a subscriber. But the choice is yours—to continue or cancel, any time at all! So why not take us up on ou invitation, with no risk of any kind. You'll be glad you did!

YOURS FREE!

This beautiful porcelain box is topped with a lovely bouquet of porcelain flowers, perfect for holding rings, pins or other precious trinkets— and is yours ABSOLUTELY FREE when you accept our NO-RISK offer!

NOT ACTUAL SIZE

NO COST! NO OBLIGATION TO BUY!
NO PURCHASE NECESSARY!

The Silhouette Reader Service™—Here's how it works

From the corner of her eye she could see the small smile tugging at his lips. Her heart sank to the pit of her stomach; he hadn't bought one lying word of what she tried to sell him.

"That was one hell of a kiss Hanlon gave your friend."

"What?" she asked, startled by his forthrightness.

"I said, it was one hell of a kiss."

"I—I don't know," she said, wetting her lower lip as she looked away from him. "It was just a kiss. Wasn't it?"

"No."

She quickly turned back to him. "No?"

Without fanfare, he cupped her face in his hands and landed a short, solid, electrifying kiss on her mouth that shot through her body clear down to her toes. "*That* was just a kiss."

Taking her in his arms, he slipped his fingers under the black velvet bands crisscrossing her back, then skimmed them down her spine. The sensation caused her to part her lips in a silent gasp, giving him what he wanted. Access to her mouth.

"On the other hand, *this* is one hell of a kiss."

He worked his mouth on hers like an expert, starting with a suctioning connection that drew on every pleasure zone on her body, and making her feel sexier than she'd ever felt. Just when she thought he'd proved his point, he ended the lip-locking seal and began a series of teasing wet nibbles that made the tips of her breasts pearl and shivery heat gather between her legs. He was right. Oh, so tummy-tickling, toe-curling, heart-hammering right. This was one hell of a kiss.

Slipping her fingers into his hair, she invited him with a well-aimed wriggle of her hips to explore the intimate recesses of her mouth.

The moment she decided to join in, Spence knew he was in for the kiss of lifetime. They worked their mouths and tongues like two hungry children with one fast-melting ice cream. They couldn't get enough and they couldn't get it fast enough. Each sweet, mouth-watering lick only made them hungrier for more.

Tangled in each other's embrace, Spencer walked her backward through dangling streamers to press her against the wall. Drifting shadows freed her further, sending her thigh up the outside of his leg. The heavenly ascent was stopped by the restraining fit of her tight dress refusing to give up an inch more of her virtue. His momentary disappointment turned to gratitude when he realized the state of his arousal. He had to back off or risk major embarrassment. Slapping his two hands against the wall on either side of her head, he gulped in enough air to speak.

"See the difference?"

Six

Jade nodded with all the grace of a stunned robot. "I... Yes, I see the difference."

"Good," Spence said with a matching nod.

Slow-motion patterns of watery light and seductive shadows filtering through the curtain of streamers were adding an erotic glow to her already mind-boggling beauty. He couldn't stop looking at her, couldn't stop wanting her and couldn't imagine a more inappropriate moment, with two hundred people several yards away, to do anything about it.

Just one more touch, he told himself as he traced the side of her satin-smooth neck with his fingertips. Nothing ever felt so soft, so feminine, so vitally inviting. He took a slow, uneven breath and considered the consequences if he kept on touching her.

They were adults. This was a public place. How

out of control could things get? He wasn't going to take her against the wall. At least, not here and not the first time. But if he didn't touch her again, at least one time, he could do serious damage to his machismo.

Lowering his head, he retraced the path his fingers had taken, but this time he delivered his touch in a skipping trail of butterfly kisses. It seemed a shame to stop when she was encouraging him to continue with those light strokes she was delivering to his hips.

Nudging the black velvet dress off one of her shoulders, he took a few tender nips at her creamy skin. Wanton shivers flurried through her, coaxing the most intriguing sounds from her throat and sending his blood thundering through his veins.

"Wh-what kind of kisses are those?"

"Custom-made ones," he said, slipping the dress back on her shoulder, "just for you." His eyes met hers and with lusty moans of surrender they gave in to the inevitable.

"Oh, Spencer," she whispered, dropping her head back in an invitation for him to continue.

"Ahh, Jade," he said, moving close.

She wound her arms around his neck as her body sought a jigsaw-tight fit with his. He felt her leg on the outside of his again and without hesitation he cupped the sides of her dress and slid the velvet high up her thighs. Okay, he could admit he was wrong. Maybe she did want him to take her against the wall. Well, if she did, he'd do his best to accommodate her. Or die a happy man trying.

Out of nowhere Megan Sloan's voice sounded over the loudspeakers and into their moment.

"This night has been filled with more surprises than any of us could have anticipated. But that's part of the fun of a high school reunion. Part of what makes a successful one. Speaking of success, I'm going to turn the microphone over to our class president and valedictorian. The person who fulfilled her class destiny. The girl voted Most Likely To Succeed, Jade Macleod."

Jade stiffened in Spence's arms as applause rolled across the gym.

"Jade?" Megan's voice boomed as the sound system squealed. "Are you out there?"

"My speech," Jade said, unwinding her leg from around his calf as she disentangled herself from his embrace.

Megan called her name again as she stepped away from Spence.

"How do I look?" she asked, smoothing flattened fingers over her cheeks then down the front of her dress as Spence gently worked her hem closer to her knees.

He straightened up and stepped back. "Let's put it this way, I'd listen to anything you had to say." When her doubtful expression didn't change, he parted the curtain of streamers and gave her a gentle shove. "Go get 'em, boss lady. You'll be terrific."

And she was. Until the end of her off-the-cuff remarks when a former classmate, teacher Rory Buchanan, took the stage and asked Jade to give her Follett River Elementary School's sixth grade pupils a tour of Capitol Hill and her office.

Spence held his breath. Since she didn't have a Capitol Hill office to show off any longer, he wondered how she was going to lie her way out of this one.

"I'll see what I can do about setting up a tour, but—"

Before she could finish her statement Rory was giving her a hug and the room was vibrating with another round of applause.

"You never disappoint us, Jade," Megan said, leading still another round of applause as the girl Most Likely To Tell Another Lie Or Two left the stage.

During the ride home Jade strained to join Neal and Casey in their hilarious recap of the evening, but her upbeat charade wasn't fooling Spence. Ever since she allowed people to believe she'd be taking the sixth grade class on that private tour, Spence was unable to get her to look him in the eye. When he stretched an arm along the back of her seat, she moved closer to her door and hastily began fashioning her hair into a French twist. Not a good sign. Neither was that sinking feeling in his chest. By the time Neal drove up to the Macleods' door, Jade was talking about locking herself in her room for the remainder of her vacation to work on several unfinished office projects.

"Does that mean Casey and I can borrow your personal assistant here for a couple of days of skiing in the Poconos?"

"Take him, please."

Spence glanced down at her lap where her fingers were laced together in a white-knuckled ball. She had no job. She had no projects. What she did have was an enormous amount of tension that had canceled out the closeness they had found behind the curtain of streamers. And what Spence had was more confusion and misgivings than ever about her guilty role in any of Sylvia Bloomfield's travel-fraud schemes. Could a person who became so tense over lying about taking children on a tour be the same person committing unethical acts in her government job?

He shook his head. "Sorry, you two, but I'll have to pass. Whether your sister wants to admit it or not, she needs me now more than ever."

"No, I don't," Jade said, reaching for the door handle.

"Yes, you do," he said, following her out of the car.

"No, I don't!" She headed up the shoveled walk toward the double-wreathed doors of the stately house.

"Yes, you do."

Casey rolled down the window and stuck out her head. "If you two decide you can get along without each other, we're leaving around six tomorrow morning."

"Got it," Spence said then headed up the walk.

By the time he'd stepped inside the house, Jade had taken off her coat and her high-heeled pumps. Clutching them to her middle, she was halfway up the stairs when he closed the door.

"Hold on. We need to talk about what happened between us."

"It's late," she said, hurrying up the stairs.

"Jade."

She turned around at the landing and looked at him for a long, lingering moment. He started up after her but she shook her head and gave an unconvincing laugh. "A little wine, a little music and before you know it, people are saying and doing the craziest things at these reunions. It's really embarrassing, isn't it?"

Before he could tell her the wine and the music had nothing to do with what happened between them, she'd disappeared into her room.

Spence saw her at breakfast the next morning for as long as it took her to pour a cup of coffee, grab a cranberry muffin and flee from the praise her parents were heaping on her about taking the schoolchildren on a tour.

"I'll be in my room most of the day working, so don't expect to see much of me," she called from the foyer.

"If you think it's necessary," Mr. Macleod called after her before turning back to his newspaper. "I don't know where she got this overdeveloped sense of dedication. Even when my company was in its early stages, I spent my vacations vacationing."

Mrs. Macleod turned to Spence who was serving himself a plate of waffles from the sideboard. "Does she seem to you to be a little distracted?"

"Yes, ma'am," he said.

Mrs. Macleod shook her head. "If Neal hadn't told us before he left on his ski trip this morning that she'd agreed to take a group of children on a tour, we probably would have had to read about it in the newspaper. You'll be helping her with that, won't you?"

Setting his plate on the table, he pulled out a chair and sat down. "I help whenever she lets me, Mrs. Macleod," he said, dropping a napkin onto his lap.

"Honestly, Spencer, I don't know where she gets the time to volunteer for these sorts of things. Sylvia Bloomfield keeps Jade so busy." The older woman's eyebrow moved upward the tiniest bit. "I wish there was something someone could do to get her to relax more."

"I'm doing my best, Mrs. Macleod," Spence said as he reached for the syrup.

"I'm sure you are, but don't give up. If I know my daughter, she needs a little extra encouragement in these matters." Mrs. Macleod gave a perfunctory glance toward the door to make sure Jade wasn't lingering there listening to their conversation. Turning back to Spencer, she leaned toward him over her plate.

"You see," she began, in a whisper this time, "it's as if she believes the only thing worth succeeding at is her career. But we know that's not true. Don't we, Spencer?"

"Yes, ma'am."

"I'm glad you agree." She tapped her fingers against her chin. "Then again, maybe I'm assuming too much. Mothers sometimes do, you know. She *could* end up finishing her work early today."

"She could," he said, wondering what the lovely woman with the strawberry blond hair and a penchant for mischief was getting at. He forked in a crisp mouthful of Belgian waffle. Whatever she was getting at, he'd bet his laptop computer that the plan involved him.

Mrs. Macleod gave a long and dramatic sigh that caused her husband to lower his newspaper and look at her. "Spencer, I was just thinking that if she does spend the entire day upstairs on that tedious paper-work, she'll be in desperate need of a break around dinnertime.''

Spencer stopped chewing and nodded.

"Unfortunately, my husband and I are going out this evening." She turned to her husband. "The Bellamys, dear. Remember?''

Mr. Macleod frowned. "How can I forget? Home videos of their trip to Malta and another recap of their fender bender with Prince what's-his-name.'' With a few colorful curses, he went back to his reading.

"We'll be leaving around six," she said, admiring the design on the handle of her spoon. She pursed her lips in concentration before widening them into a daz-zling smile, as if a new idea had suddenly come to her. Looking up at Spence, she said, "Perhaps you could look in on her?''

As he headed for Jade's door a little past six that evening, Spence reminded himself, despite Mrs. Macleod's thinly veiled prompting otherwise, that this was strictly a courtesy visit. Sure, he'd earned an im-pressive reputation over the years for using every trick in the book in pursuit of a story, but he'd be damned if he would ever use the same tactics in pur-suit of a woman. Especially Jade. Distressed and con-fused as she appeared to be, he would deserve a one-finger salute from every decent male in the country if he offered her more than a friendly shoulder tonight. On the other hand, if she wanted to talk about Sylvia Bloomfield, he'd be the first to encourage her.

He knocked on her door. "Are you all right in there?''

"Yes, but I'm busy.''

"Prove it."

He heard several soft footsteps before she opened the door. "You're not known for your subtleties, are you?"

"Hey, it beats lying," he said, pointedly looking at the wad of tissues in her hand and then at her red-rimmed eyes. He shook his head as he took in her hair, most of which had made wild and daring escapes from her topknot during the day.

"What do you mean, 'lying'?"

"You don't look busy," he said, as his gaze slid over her clingy, black sweater with the top three buttons undone, and a pair of clutching, cupping jeans he was instantly jealous of.

"What do you want, Spencer?" she asked as she stuffed the tissues in her pocket and tucked a coil of curly hair behind her ear.

"Neal's gone skiing. Your parents went out for the evening." He lifted the supper tray in his hands. "I didn't want to eat alone."

She leaned a hip against the door, considered him for all of two seconds then sighed and waved him in. "Leave the lights off. My eyes are sore from... reading all day."

"Sure," he said setting the tray on her desk. "What'll it be? Roast beef and rosé or peanut butter and bacon and rosé?" Reaching for a glass, he began pouring the wine he'd uncorked in the kitchen a few minutes before.

In spite of her hesitant attitude at the door, she managed a small smile. "Who told you that pb&b's are my second choice in comfort food after Smoochies?" she asked, picking up a sandwich plate.

He handed her a half-filled glass of wine. "Sorry, I always protect my sources."

"Thanks," she said, watching him for a moment before heading for the love seat.

A few seconds later he walked in front of the love seat, a roast beef sandwich in one hand and a wineglass in the other. "Interesting atmosphere you have going here," he said, gesturing with his hand that held the sandwich. He indicated the darkened room lit only with the scented candle he'd given her. "What do you call it? Country French catacomb? Or upscale Bat Cave?"

She swallowed a mouthful of sandwich then set the plate on the end table. "I was taking a break when you knocked. With the lights off, it's very peaceful watching the snow falling on the back garden."

"Really?" He took the space beside her on the love seat. "The snow stopped an hour ago."

"I meant…I was—"

"Crying, Jade," he said softly. "You were crying."

She pushed up from the cushion and walked over to the glass doors leading out to the balcony. "Look, I'm having a bad day. Okay?"

"Hmm. Does this have something to do with that box of tampons you had me buy?"

Flattening her hands against the glass, she let her forehead thunk against it and gave in to weak laughter. "That was last week."

"I see," he said, pushing off the cushion and crossing the few feet to where she stood. As he reached the glass door, she leaned away from him to press her shoulder against the doorjamb. *Hey, don't be afraid. Talk to me, kiddo. Talk to me about anything. Your career. Your ex-boyfriend. Those kisses we shared last night.* He closed his eyes for a second. *Don't even think about going down that road, Spence, ol' boy.*

Shifting her weight, Jade pressed her hip against the doorjamb and crossed her arms. The change in her position accentuated her full breasts and outlined her already peaked nipples. Her sweater had flapped open near the top where those three buttons were undone, exposing a creamy curve of skin that begged for his... She looked at him. He looked away and ran his fingers through his hair. *Give it a break, Spence. She's not lusting after you, she's just standing near a window on a very cold night.* He scratched his head. *Right, sure, but if it's so damn cold, why are you feeling so distinctly aroused yourself?* He had no snappy retort for that, just a pleasant ache in his groin.

He cleared his throat, as he tried to think of another subject. "Pretty moon."

She shrugged and slid her hands into her jean pockets.

"I guess. But I've always thought these picture-perfect moons were overrated."

Turning slowly toward her, he rested his shoulder against the glass and slipped his hands in his jeans to mirror her stance. "You want to run that by me again?"

"When it comes to romance..."

"Romance?" He teased her with his eyes.

"It's as unnoticeable as a lighted billboard up there," she said, accidentally banging her fingers on

the window when she attempted to point at the sky.
"Like a blinking neon sign demanding attention...forcing you to talk about it as if it were an
object of divine inspiration instead of what it
is...which is just a rock that gets between you and
the sun every now and then." She finished up her
rambling speech by sticking the finger she'd banged
the hardest into her mouth.

"So you'd prefer total darkness when you're alone
with a man?"

Slowly pulling out her finger, she blew on its glistening tip. "I didn't say that."

Spence stared at her finger, fighting the temptation
to ask her if he could suck it, too. Instead, he frowned.
"What would you prefer?"

"Actually, I, uh, well..." Her chest heaved with
her next breath. "I prefer starry skies. I think they're
more conducive to a romantic mood," she said before
biting down on her lower lip to stop it from quivering.

If he didn't stop her soon, he was going to forget
all about staying away from her and give her the longest, deepest, wettest kiss she'd ever had and he'd ever
given.

"Right," he said in a painfully patient voice as he
held his hands, palms up, between them. "That's really interesting, but you'd be doing us a favor if you
would just back up and tell me what's been eating at
you."

A moment before, Jade's heart felt as light as an
untethered balloon floating freely, if not a little hesitantly, around the room. One slingshot sentence from
Spencer and it was lying in pieces on the floor. Lord,
would she ever learn that she wasn't femme-fatale

material and never would be. She fixed her stare to a shadowy corner of the room.

"I've been missing Richard."

Spence shook his head. "You've missed your car more than you've missed him."

She blinked nervously then gave him a guilty look. "Okay. It's just been a bad day."

"This has nothing to do with one bad day. You've been in panic-alert status since before our train pulled into town. You snap at me every time I turn around. And when you do start to relax with me, something comes over you and you clam up. Now you've got yourself holed up in your room avoiding that incredibly loving family of yours so that you can be alone to cry. Over what? Jade, what is going on?"

Jade twisted her fingers into her hair and shook her head. "Go away," she said, feeling her lips beginning to quiver again. "You have no right to push like this."

He took hold of her wrists and when she let go of her hair, he slowly pulled them to his chest. "I have the right because I am your friend. Jade, I'm not letting go of you until you tell me what is going on."

She looked up at the ceiling and gave a sigh of resignation. "All right, I give up. What is going on is what is *not* going on."

Spencer squinted then lifted his chin. "You want to hit me with that again?"

She took the opportunity to slide her wrists from his grip, jam her hands to her hips and sink her backside against the wall. "You asked for it. You know that class of sixth graders I'm supposed to be taking on a tour of my office?"

"Yes?"

"Spence, I'm not taking anyone on a tour of my office because I don't have an office. I've been fired. Let go. Kicked out on my can. There. Are you happy now?"

"Are you?"

"Do I look happy?"

"You looked pissed."

"I am!" she said loudly and indignantly. "I did *not* deserve to be treated like that!"

"Finally. I think we've hit a vein."

"Yes, a big nasty one," she said with an emphatic shake of her hands. "Oh, Spencer, I'm so tired of holding this in. And you've been so patient putting up with me when I didn't deserve it. What am I ever going to do to make things up to you?"

"It's not a problem. Just get it all out," he said with a deep shrug. "Let it rip, kiddo."

"All right. I think she should have fired Lance."

"Lance?"

"Lance Barclay. He used to be Sylvia's personal fitness trainer, now he's her protégé and special assistant. Around the office the rest of us referred to him as the phantom because he hardly ever shows his face there. But the Saturday night before I came up to Follett River, he showed more than his face, if you know what I mean."

Spence felt his ears perk up. Sylvia Bloomfield engaged in a little hanky-panky with her young, male assistant? This kind of information was exactly what he needed for his article; the flip side of a professionally produced, perfectly polished image.

"Lance showed more than his face?" he asked with a deadpan expression. "What do you mean?"

Her straight-on stare suddenly started skipping around the room. "You know."

"He was...rude to you?"

"He's always rude to me." She repositioned her backside against the wall. "But nothing like the way he was that night." She looked away as if she couldn't bear to meet his eyes.

"You're doing fine."

"I walked into Sylvia's office and found the both of them on top of her desk." She made a skittering motion with her hands. "You can imagine the rest of it. And they both acted as if I was the one doing something wrong."

Even as her anger began building again, Spence felt like taking her in his arms and dancing her around the room. Of course, then he would have to explain why. His jubilant mood dropped several notches when he thought about the trust she'd placed in him and the plans he had for it.

Narrowing her eyes, Jade slapped her hand against her chest. "It makes me crazy when I think about it. A highly respected, married, twice-elected official, a woman who has cultivated the public's trust, doing something so tawdry, so dishonest, so self-centered as to keep a paid lover on staff when there are some women out there who have never had an orgasm. Well, it's true, Spencer, because I saw it. And because of her influence up on the Hill, she was only too happy to make it clear to me that if I went public with what I discovered, it would be her word against mine."

Opening his mouth, Spence motioned for her to stop.

"Wait. I'm not finished. So now I'm without a job. And Sylvia is now being bold, angry or stupid enough to send me on my way without a decent letter of reference." Jade stomped her foot on the floor. "Can you believe all this?"

Spence scratched the space between his brows with his thumbnail.

"Well, can you?"

"Everything except the part about you never having had an orgasm."

Jade lived up to the curse of every fair-skinned, redhead he'd ever known when two scarlet stains blazed below her cheekbones like an out-of-control wildfire. Staring straight ahead she struggled to crank up one side of her lips into a half smile.

"D-did I say that?"

He nodded. "Yeah. Right after the part about keeping a paid lover—"

"Well," she cut in, blinking as if her nerve endings had suddenly short-circuited. "It's not important. I mean, there's not a colored ribbon to wear for...that. It's just one of those things I haven't gotten around to yet," she said, before squinching up her lips. "You know, people make way too much of sex. Look at Sylvia and Lance. No, wait!" Her gaze landed dead center on his. "I didn't mean that the way it sounded. Oh, could you please forget I mentioned it."

Scarlet stains were creeping down her neck about the same time he realized her failure to achieve sexual fulfillment bothered her more than being fired. As she lowered her head, Spence's heart went with it.

He pressed a hand to the wall beside her face and lifted her chin on his crooked fingers. "Hey, your secret's safe with me, kiddo." When she refused to meet his eyes, he softened his voice further. "You can trust me on this one," he said as ripping guilt tore at his insides. *This one, Jade, but not the rest of it.*

After several seconds, her gold-tipped lashes swept upward until her eyes met his. There were no darting movements this time, no sliding glances to the side and no unfocused stare. What he saw was a straight-on honesty that made his heart pound. "Jade, no one has to know."

"You know," she said.

Seven

———

The journalist's part of Spence's mind instructed him to steer the conversation back around to the shenanigans in Representative Bloomfield's office. But questions about Lance Barclay's job qualifications, the number and destinations of trips he'd taken with the congresswoman and the time he'd spent working in the office were going to have to wait because as Spence looked into Jade's eyes, his heart was telling him something completely different.

Fragile. Handle with extreme care.

"Not many women are brave enough or honest enough to admit what you just did."

"Please," Jade said, hitting him with a crooked smile that turned one part of him to jelly and another part to stone. "No applause." Ducking under his arm, she walked several steps away from him. "I hadn't planned to share that with anyone. Ever."

"But you shared it with me. You want to talk about it?"

She kept her back to him and shrugged.

"I'll listen as a friend, Jade. No judging, no making you feel any worse than you already do."

She looked over her shoulder and blinked those big baby blues at him. His heart swelled in his chest. She was in pain and he was in deep trouble this time. Once she started to talk—*if* she started—he knew damn well he would end up wanting to offer her more of himself than a sympathetic ear. While he still had a chance to back away, he was going to take it. "Jade?"

Her head down, her palms grinding against each other, she began turning around.

"If you think you'll be too uncomfortable—"

Her words burst out on top of his own. "Maybe there's something wrong with me."

"Oh, I doubt it," he said lightly as he silently counted the steps to the door.

"You're just saying that to make me feel better, but something—" she splayed her fingers in frustration "—something important is missing."

"There's nothing wrong with you."

"Then I must be *doing* something wrong. I've read every self-help sex manual there is. I've done everything they told me to. Believe me," she said, rolling her eyes and shaking her head, "I've followed all the instructions to the letter."

Her guileless expression and earnest stare affected him more than anything else she could have said. He swallowed slowly, guiltily relishing the aftertaste of his quick surrender to the inevitable role as her confessor. "Can you be a little more specific?"

"Oh, why not?" Her gaze flittered back and forth between him and nowhere. "I can't possibly embarrass myself any more than I already have."

Spence knew the testy sigh that followed her words was there to counter her growing self-consciousness. He guessed she still needed a little more time. Fine, he thought, walking over to the end table and picking up his wineglass. He could use a little time himself to regroup. Before he had finished filling his mouth with rosé, the dam began to burst.

"I think everything is going along the way it should and then, right at that point," she said, striking her fist against her palm, "when...well, you know, when bells should start ringing and fireworks exploding, I tense up. I quit. And quitting is not my style." She started pacing the room. "Maybe I'm overanalyzing, but I keep coming back to one explanation."

He raised his brows.

"I think I need my reset button pushed."

He coughed on his wine, then swiped at his chin as he set his glass aside. "Your reset button... pushed?"

"Right. It's as if I've been heading toward a cliff and when I start to close in on the edge, I suddenly lose my nerve. The craziest thoughts run through my mind. What if I lose control? What if I keep on falling and there's no one there to catch me? What if that's all there is, just a leap to nowhere?"

He plowed his fingers through his hair. "Have you ever talked about this to...uh—?"

"Heavens, no," she said, looking around the floor

for the proverbial trapdoor of escape. "I couldn't. That would be admitting I—I—"

"Faked it?"

"Yes." Jade seemed to shrink inches before his eyes. "Oh, why did I agree to talk about this?" she asked, covering her face with her hands. "I should have written to that advice columnist like I'd planned—"

"It's okay," he said, coming across the room to smooth his hands over her shoulders. "Look, I'm no sex therapist, but it sounds as if part of this problem could be your choice in partners."

"There have been only two. Almost three, but he got ahead of things and..." She dropped her hands and looked up. "Is that it? Is it that I'm not experienced enough? Because if that's the answer, then this mother of all confessions has been a big mistake. I'm a very discriminating person."

Spence had nobly pretended to himself that he could be an understanding presence for Jade while she emptied her heart of self-doubt and bad experiences. The time for pretending was over; her teary, desperate voice was a clarion call for him to get real.

"Of course, you're discriminating," he said, taking her in his arms the way he should have the second he walked in. She fit as perfectly to him tonight as she had when they'd danced. But this time they were alone, he thought, sliding his hands to the inviting curve of her waist. Gently swaying her, he lingered against the trembling warmth of her body in the expectant silence of their embrace.

"It only takes one man, Jade."

Pulling back in his arms, Jade looked up at him as she began twisting one of his shirt buttons.

"I'd like to think that, but deep down I wonder what any man can expect from someone who wears flannel pajamas."

"The right man," he said, looking her over, "can expect to help her out of those flannel pajamas when the time comes to make love. He can listen to her, take his time with her...a long time, if that's what it takes to get in tune with her body. Jade, the way you succeed in a career is not the way you succeed at something as intimate as making love. If you're with someone who cares enough, he'll do his damnedest to make you feel as if you're the most wonderful person that ever came into his life. Then there shouldn't be a reason to analyze what felt wrong because everything will feel right."

Spence drew his fingers over her arms. It took all of his control not to pop open that button she was playing with, strip off his shirt and begin making love to her. But instinct told him she would have to be the one to take the next step. He removed her hand from his shirt front and stepped back. "Those others have sold you short, Jade Macleod."

"They have? A-about what?"

"In or out of flannel pajamas, you're an incredibly desirable woman." As he waited for her response he began to wonder where all the oxygen in the room had disappeared to.

"And you think the right man could prove that?" she asked, a trace of doubt lingering in her eyes.

"When you're ready, *you* and the right man could prove it together." Smiling, he started for the door.

"Spence. Wait."

He stopped halfway across the room, thought about saying a prayer but decided in the same second to turn around instead. The moment shimmered in the candlelit room.

She nibbled at her bottom lip. "Do you think I was ready for those kisses we shared at the reunion?"

He thought back to the eager way she'd responded to his kisses, wrapping her leg around his, nudging herself against his growing erection. He managed a nod. "Oh, yeah."

"And you weren't kissing me because you felt sorry for me, were you?" she asked, her brave and needy look reaching to the center of his heart.

He crossed the room in three strides, took her in his arms and drank her in with his eyes. "Ah, cripes. Sorry had nothing to do with those kisses. Jade, they were real. As real as this." Wrapping his fingers around her hair, he brought her face close to his and pressed his lips to hers in a hot, probing kiss. When he was through, he leaned his forehead against hers. "Any more questions?"

She nodded. "Will you make love to me?"

His answer was another heart-stopping, knee-weakening kiss. "Jade, asking me to make love to you is like asking water to flow over Niagara," he said, with enough heartfelt emotion to make his voice hoarse with need. "I want to satisfy every desire you've ever had. I want to be the one to make those bells ring and those fireworks explode inside you. There's nothing wrong that we can't make right together."

"I'm so happy you said that," she whispered as he kissed her fingers, one by one.

"I'm even happier that you asked," he said before they shared a tender laugh. "We've got all night, Jade, and we're going to enjoy it for as long as we can."

Her eyes widened with a teasing look of shock and surprise.

"Quickly," he said, "tell me what you're thinking right now."

"I'm thinking, all my life I've tried living down my exotic name, but with you all I want to do is live up to it."

"Exotic. All right," he said, nodding slowly as he put his plan together. "Pull out that pack of relaxation tapes I gave you and slip the rain forest one into your tape deck. Then meet me in the bathroom and bring that candle with you."

When she opened her mouth, he pressed his fingers to her lips. "Trust me?"

She gave him a sexy smile that nearly paralyzed him, then whispered, "I do."

By the time she pushed open the door to the bathroom, Spence had found her unopened container of Mango Tango bubble bath, cracked the seal and poured a capful under a stream of running bathwater. He clicked off the light switch.

"Sorry I couldn't bring the stars in here," he said, taking the candle from her and setting it on the sink. "Will candlelight do?"

"It's perfect.

"Good," he said, as he slipped his fingers beneath the bottom edge of her sweater then pulled it off over her head. "Because it's come to my attention, Miss Macleod, that no one has ever properly seduced you." He tossed her sweater on the floor, turned off the water and took a seat on the rim of the big oval tub. Wriggling his fingers, he urged her closer with a smile.

Jade stepped into the sprawling space he'd made for her between his legs. As she reached for his shoulders, a screeching birdcall from the rain forest tape made her gasp and pull her hands away.

"Hey. How's that for exotic?"

They both laughed as she settled her hands on his shoulders. "Pretty authentic," she said as he reached for the front closure on her bra.

She looked away while he pushed the cotton cups aside.

"I'm afraid if sexy underwear is a requirement, I've got a long way to go."

He slid the plain white bra down her arms and tossed it on the sweater. Looking up at her, he gave her a reassuring wink then began to lightly rub his palms against the tips of her breasts. She felt pleasure from his touch all the way to her thighs. "That's wonderful," she whispered as she ran her fingers through his hair. When he tongued the pearling red tip of one breast, she suddenly felt a need to start breathing through her mouth.

"You're wonderful," he said, gently teasing the wet, distended flesh with his thumb. "I can't imagine any man not wanting to take his time with you."

The persistent touch of his thumb followed by the delicate stroke of his tongue had her squeezing her thighs together, as she tried gathering her thoughts to speak.

"Talk to me, Jade. Ask me for less. Ask me for more."

"That's fine. What you're doing is fine."

"But it's not enough, is it?"

She shook her head.

"How did I know that?" he asked as he drew his fingers over her rib cage.

"I don't know," she said in a rushing whisper.

"Because I'm taking my time. Because I'm asking you," he said as he began drawing his thumb back and forth across the jean-covered space between her legs. "Because I care." He moved his fingers higher on her cleft, concentrating his exquisite attention on the pulsing flesh beneath the material. "Is this better?"

The deep and immediate pleasure was startling in its intensity. She sucked in air then let it out in a sigh as she moved against his thumb. Just when she was about to tell him how turned-on he made her feel, he took his hand away, unsnapped her jeans and slowly lowered her zipper.

He looked up with a knowing smile. "Wiggle your hips for me. Nice and slow, that's it," he said, as he hooked his thumbs over the waistband and began lowering her jeans and panties. When he'd worked them to the tops of her thighs, he held her still to trail kisses over the flat plane of her belly.

She reached to sink her fingers into his hair, but by then he'd already taken his mouth away and was working her jeans and panties to her ankles. When she stepped out of them and started for the sanctuary of the bubbles, he held her at arm's length.

"Not so fast." His lazy stare covered her from head to toe and back again. "I've waited a long time for this. Turn around for me. Slowly. I want to look at you...every bit of you."

His hot stare continued as heightening sensations tingled through her. The naked desire in his eyes only added to the powerful need growing within her.

"When you look at me like that, it's like you're touching me. Here," she said, brazenly drawing one hand over her breasts. "And here," she said. "Especially here." The tips of her fingers barely touched the red-gold thatch of hair at the apex of her thighs, but his hot, steady stare didn't miss a move.

As much as he appeared to be in control, she sensed that her bold words and provocative touches were exciting him when he rubbed at his mouth and shook his head. He reached for her hands.

"Are you coming in?" she asked, her heart fluttering as he helped her over the rim.

"No. This bath is for you. Besides, I've already had two showers today," he said taking off his shirt and tossing it on the growing pile of discarded clothing as he watched her sink into the fragrant bubbles.

Kneeling beside the tub, he began washing her with long, languid strokes, smoothing the tangy-scented bubbles down her neck and across her shoulders. Lifting her arm, he swirled the creamy froth along to her wrist and then turned her hand over and washed her palm. The sound of birdcalls and pattering rain from the tape filled the room. If that wasn't making the atmosphere sultry enough, the words he began to whisper about the feel of her and what it was doing to his manhood did. While he nuzzled her neck, he ran one hand down her back and the other over her breasts. Lingering at her rosy tips, he used both hands to make exquisitely slow circles around them with the frothy lather.

"No one has ever taken such thorough care with me," she whispered, weaving her shoulders in invitation for more. When his slow play continued, she pressed forward to fill his hands with her breasts. Instead of a firmer caress, he trailed his hands down her midriff.

"I plan on taking thorough care of every inch of you," he said, as he reached below the bubbles into the water. Running his hand up the inside of her thighs, he gently parted them while he dropped light kisses against her temple. "Turn toward me."

Twisting on her hip, she planted a foot on the bottom of the tub and closed one hand over the rim to steady herself. His fingers continued drifting over the tops of her thighs. "You're touching me as if I'm going to break." She kissed his chin and then his mouth. "I won't break," she said, but her voice did as he slid his finger inside the delicate folds of her feminine flesh.

When Spence felt a squeeze of wet satin around his finger, his body reacted as if the tight caress had been around his manhood. He plunged deeper and suddenly she was holding her breath then pushing him away.

"Too much, too soon?" he asked as the sexual excitement he'd seen building in her suddenly appeared to collapse under a splash of scented water.

"I—yes," she said, tension apparent in her startled voice and wrinkled brow. "I didn't mean to jerk away like that." She gulped air. "I'm sorry."

"For what?" he asked, resting his wrists on the rim as he searched her disappointed expression. "Now I just know to take it slower." He smiled as he waited for a sign to continue, but her look of embarrassment only worsened. "Jade?"

She did her best to smile back but her attempt failed miserably. She looked away. He waited, continuing to watch her as he kept his hands above the waterline. After several more seconds had passed, he leaned in to plant a kiss on the tip of her nose. He repeated the act twice more.

"Where is that reset button you told me about? Here?" He kissed her nose one more time before moving his lips to her earlobe. He kept on kissing her there, bathing the delicate pink shell with his tongue until she was hunching her shoulder. "Maybe here?"

"Keep doing that," she said, fighting back a whisper of a laugh. "I think you're getting closer to it."

"I'm getting closer to something," he said, referring to his own state of arousal. He braced his hands against the tub, took a few calming breaths, and after a few seconds stood up. Helping her to her feet, he rinsed the soapy remains of the bubble bath from her body, then helped her out onto the rug. Scooping her up into his arms, he headed for the connecting door to his bedroom.

"I'm not dry," she protested.

"I know," he said, awkwardly working the doorknob then giving the door a push with his knee. "But this is exactly the way I want you."

"What way?" She circled her slippery arms around his neck.

"Wet. Warm. Smelling like forbidden fruit," he said, crossing the room to settle her on the bed. Resting his hands on either side of her hips, he leaned close to take stock of the pink blush covering her face. Smiling to himself, he knew his sexual teasing was as much to blame for her coloring as the temperature of the bath.

"You might as well know this, too. I've thought about you curled around me in this bed every night since I arrived."

Her eyes widened as he stood up, ripped down his zipper and began shoving off the rest of his clothes. "And when I picked out the bubble bath, and the rest of it, my fantasies about you got a bit fancier."

"I inspired fantasies for you?" she asked in a disbelieving whisper. Pulling the sheet between her legs, she faced away from him. "Honest? You wanted me then?"

Closing his hands around her arms, he kneeled onto the bed. "More than a Smoochie," he teased, then pulled her back against the length of him to feel the delicious vibrations of her laughter. He turned her around to face him.

"Every night, Jade," he said, his tone undeniably serious this time, as he lifted a wet curl away from her neck, looped it around his fingertip then gently released the springy red coil. The slow-motion ballet continued as beads of water rolled down the pale column of her neck and into the satiny space between her breasts. "Every morning," he whispered, as he caught a drop on his finger and brought it to his lips. "All the time. I've ached to be with you like this."

She pressed her hand against his mat of chest hair.

"Have I said too much? I'll slow down, if you want," he said, knowing if he went any slower he'd probably have a heart attack.

Shaking her head slowly, she lifted his hand to her mouth and licked the finger he'd just had at his lips. "Don't slow down," she said, stringing a line of butterfly kisses across his chest before lowering her hands to stroke her thighs.

"Tell me what you want, Jade."

"I...I want more."

"Of what?" he whispered, reaching to skim his fingers beneath the red-gold thatch of hair between her thighs. "Go on," he said, skimming closer to her slick heat this time. "You can tell me."

She moved her hands faster up and down her thighs. "You," she said, clutching her knees when his finger came dangerously close to entry. "Oh, Spencer." She closed her eyes and dropped her head on his shoulder as he began to delicately stroke her satiny nub of feminine flesh. "You...kn-know my body better than I do." She licked at her lips, opened her eyes and reached for him. Wrapping her hand around his firm, hot flesh, she smoothed her thumb over the drop of moisture at its tip. "I want more of you."

Pushing her hand away, he pressed her back on the pillows, then lowered his lips to taste her. She moved against him, as moans of escalating pleasure broke in her throat. Clutching at the sheet, her thighs brushed his cheeks and she began to writhe beneath his mouth.

Her feminine flesh quivered from one last stroke of his tongue the moment he sensed her coming close to release. Bracing himself above her, he moved his hips between her legs, careful not to touch her anywhere.

"Is that what you wanted?" he asked, hanging on to his own control with tortured determination.

Moving restlessly beneath him, she strained to make contact—any contact—with his body. "No," she said, rubbing his arms and then his hips. "Yes. I mean, I wanted more of you."

"How much more?"

"The rest of you. Please."

It took all his concentration not to sink into her sweet, slick heat when he nudged his swollen tip against her entrance. He repeated the action, barely penetrating her this time. "Like that?" he asked, as a fine film of perspiration broke out on his forehead.

"No, no," she said, "that's not enough. It's not enough." Her voice had taken on a frantic edge as she raised her hips in a blatant bid for him to enter her.

"Show me," he said, his voice raspy as he held back. "Guide me in, Jade. Take me deep."

She let go of his arms to wrap her hands around his hips and pull him in. He resisted at first but that only excited her more.

"You've got to want me more than that," he said, easing out of her.

She pulled him in halfway this time, but he was too strong for her, easing out when he felt her tightening around his shaft.

"I do. I want you so badly," she said, lifting her hips to feel him close. But not close enough. Not nearly close enough. As she struggled to pull him all the way in, the first shimmer of pleasure ribboned through her. She began to call his name.

"That's it," he whispered against her ear as he gave himself to her, inch by inch.

And then he was hers. All hers.

Jade set the pace, guiding him with her lightest touch, urging him faster with the tiniest sigh, until he seemed to know exactly what she wanted when she wanted it. Desire coiled tighter as he reached beneath her, lifted her hips and, with each hard thrust, whispered dark, sweet words of encouragement to her. His voice sent hot ribbons of sublime sensations whipping through her. And when that old hint of panic began to whisper in the back of her mind, Spencer's words were soft commands she was compelled to obey.

"Look at me. I'll be there. Let go. I'll catch you, Jade. Just let go."

Looking into the most tender, trustful, passion-filled eyes she'd ever seen, she suddenly began to soar. A few seconds later she was tumbling wildly through the heaven of his embrace, crying out as she felt herself fragmenting into a million stars. And through it all he continued whispering her name as if it were a magic chant. When his own climax came, it shuddered through her, taking her again through a shower of exploding stars with the most exquisite cry she'd ever heard. Whether it was from her lips or Spencer's, she couldn't say and didn't care.

They clung to each other until their hearts slowed their pounding and she could breathe and talk at the same time. But when she opened her mouth to speak, no words came.

With breathless laughter, he rolled her to his side and kissed her brow. "I never doubted," he said, holding her close as the unmistakable scent of Mango Tango bubble bath and the exotic essence of their lovemaking blended around them. He kissed her softly this time, whispering against her mouth. "Not for a second."

Eight

Bands of morning sunlight poured through the mini-blinds, striping their naked bodies with sunlight and shadows. Spence curved his hand over her hip, playing his fingers through the exotic pattern as he considered the question Jade jarred him awake with. He watched her face as her gaze shifted back and forth between his slow hand and, what he knew must be, his sleep-softened features.

"Spencer, it's a simple question. Do you or do you not agree that we went a little faster than average?" Jade asked for the second time.

His muzziness began to clear with each pass of his hand over her incredibly smooth skin. He gave her a lazy smile as he started massaging her hipbone with his thumb. "I agree, but you have to admit that in the end you were the one insisting I speed things along."

Biting her lip to keep from laughing, Jade took him by the shoulders and gave him a gentle yet exaggerated shake. "I am not talking about when we were actually making love."

"You're not?"

He rubbed sleep from his eyes before returning to the tactile pleasures of stroking her body. This time he concentrated on the curve of one breast and the delicious angle of its upturned tip.

"You want to catch me up on this conversation?" he asked, all his attention concentrated on the amazing way her body responded to his touch. "Because I'm not exactly sure what we're talking about."

"I'm talking about how short a time we've known each other. About how little we know about each other's lives."

As guilt, like an unwelcome thunderstorm, strayed into the bright morning, his hand drifted down to the sheet, still warm from where they'd lain together. Clearing his throat, he pinched at the bridge of his nose to hide his wince. Reality was biting hard this morning.

Last night Jade had bared more than her body to him; she'd bared the secrets of her heart. Because of placing that degree of trust in him, she had a reason and a right to expect the same from him. He sighed; if it were simply that easy, but it wasn't.

He'd had his fair share of lovers but none had moved him, none had touched his heart like this woman. Continuing to hold back the truth from her had become his biggest challenge. No matter how loving, how intimate they'd quickly become with each other, he still didn't know how she would react to finding out that he'd set her up to spill her guts on the less-than-honorable Sylvia Bloomfield.

And now that he was certain her pride, and not corruption, had kept her silent, the new and tender state of their deepening relationship had him choking on his deception. If he wanted to be certain of gaining more information for his exposé he couldn't take the chance of coming clean about his agenda just yet.

The only hope he had of untangling the mess he had created was to wait until she'd given him more solid evidence for his article. Before that happened, he hoped to lead her to the conclusion that some kind of action should be taken about Sylvia Bloomfield. Then he could explain about his own derailed career and she would hopefully be moved to forgive him for what he'd done. Surely because of her concerns over her own career she would be more understanding about him wanting to regain and continue his.

Spence looked her squarely in the eyes and saw enough apprehension to make his lying heart cringe. Who was he trying to kid? She was definitely not thinking about her career this morning.

"Spencer, are you having second thoughts about what happened last night...and those two times after that?"

"Never," he said, taking her hand in his. "I'll never regret a moment of it."

"Neither will I," she said, pouring a little more sunshine into the room with a soft touch and her dazzling smile. "You helped me discover something so rich, so fine.... I was starting to think it would never happen. But from the start you were right."

"About what?"

"You said it would only take one caring man. I'm so glad I trusted you," she said, sliding her leg around his hips as she brought his hand against her breasts. "All I was trying to say before was that we need time to get to know each other."

While she was poised to give him the unabridged version of her life, most of which he already knew, he was manufacturing a past based on half-truths and outright lies. To add to the ever-complicated mess, he was lying beside her, naked, unable to stop thinking about how complete she made him feel when she was in his arms.

He didn't want to think about the niggling guilt. Not for a little while, he told himself as he leaned back on the pillow, folded his hands behind his head and began to lose himself in the loving look in her eyes.

"So what are you saying, kiddo?" he asked with as much lightheartedness as he could work into his voice. "We should pretend that last night didn't happen and start over?"

"I didn't say that," she said, smiling as she stirred her fingers down through his thick mat of chest hair to where it whorled around his navel. "If we pretended last night never happened, then we'd have to pretend this morning wasn't happening."

Desire was already building within him by the time she allowed her fingers to stray across the flat plane of his belly. When she wrapped her hand around him, all he could think about was feeling more of her wrapped around more of him. His breathing deepened as she began slow, even strokes.

"And then we'd have to forget this was happening...."

"Hell of a thought," he managed to say before pressing his shoulders into the pillow and holding his breath.

"But I am right, you know. We have so much more to learn about each other."

He exhaled sharply. "I can't argue...th-there," he said, reaching for her.

"Spencer, you don't think I'm overanalyzing again, do you?"

"Yes, but it's one of your most endearing qualities," he said, as he pulled her astride his hips. "That and those sounds you make right before those bells start ringing and those fireworks start going off." Adjusting himself beneath her, he asked, "So, dinner...tonight...the Hotel Maxwell?"

"I'd love to," she said, centering herself over his burgeoning hardness. "What time?"

Gritting his teeth, he waited for her to ease down on him.

She took him in with a smile and one silky glide of a move.

"Early," he said as she began to pump her hips. "I'll, uh...come early."

"Please," she said, bracing her hands on his shoulders as her expression turned to one of surprise and then of sweet agony.

"Please what?" he asked, suddenly realizing that their casual foreplay had readied her more quickly then she'd expected. Curving his hands around her waist he speeded their movements.

She pressed her ripe lips against his, her kisses

bouncing off his mouth as she tried to speak. "Oh, Spencer," she managed to whisper as she tightened her satin center around his manhood. "Please don't...come...too early."

"I won't," he said, praying his raspy-sounding vow wouldn't prove to be another lie. The provocative rhythm of her hips had turned into a strong and steady tattoo calling out to a fresh, new place inside of him. Barely able to hold back the escalation of his own wrenching pleasure, he managed, "Now?"

"Now, Spencer. Now. Yes, oh, yes, now."

The chilled champagne was poured, the waiter had withdrawn and in the privacy of the dining room at the Hotel Maxwell, Spencer was playfully kissing her fingers.

"Talk to me, Spencer."

"Sorry," he said, "my mouth is too busy adoring you. You talk to me."

"What else do you want to know? I've already filled you in on my college years, my trip to Italy with my two girlfriends, one of whom has since become a nun, and if I give you any more details about my responsibilities as Sylvia Bloomfield's aide, she could hire you to replace me...if she hadn't already replaced me."

"Work for that saccharine-coated spider? From what you've told me, I wouldn't want to get anywhere near that sticky web of hers."

Jade reached for her champagne glass, drawing her finger up and down the stem.

"You know, Spencer, it wasn't all bad. I believe

we accomplished a lot of good work when she wasn't running off on one of her trips.''

"Sounds like you didn't get to go on a lot of them."

She shrugged. "There have been so many. I actually made quite a few of them with her."

"She worked you hard, did she?" he asked, picking up his champagne without letting go of her hand.

"I worked myself hard," she said, recalling one project in particular. "She had us traveling to this little island off the coast of Florida three times in one three-month period. Sylvia wanted a preliminary study done on a possible site for a new naval air station. That was around the time she hired Lance. Personally, I never thought much of what Sylvia insisted we call Project Suntan. And I agreed."

"Why not?"

"The area was already built up with expensive resorts and million-dollar vacation homes. Generally with that sort of situation, the locals band together and fight with all the influence they've got. Out of the blue she decided to give the project to Lance."

Spencer made a sympathetic face of skepticism. "After you worked on it? What reason did she give you?"

"She said Lance needed to start in the middle of something in order to catch on faster. Personally," Jade said, setting aside her champagne, "I thought the project was headed for the tubes and had already told her so. Maybe that was part of the reason she wanted Lance to take it over."

Spencer lifted her chin on his fingers and smiled. "So even though you knew he'd been her personal trainer without any background in congressional work, you wanted to give him a chance to prove himself?''

"Sure. Wouldn't you? Oh, Spencer, don't look at me like that. I'm not a saint. I just wanted to play fair." She shook her head. "Back then I figured that if he was going to be part of the team, Lance should have a good whack at it so I turned over everything on Project Suntan to him."

"You mean you have no records of that boondoggle."

"Boondoggle?" She squinted. "That's an interesting way of putting it, but the answer to that is no. I even gave him my computer disks," she said as Spencer nodded slowly and thoughtfully.

"So, how *did* our Mr. Barclay do with Project Suntan? Did he prove himself to be a capable assistant? I mean, away from her desktop."

"Gee, Mr. Madison," she said, batting her lashes. "I just love it when you talk snotty like that."

Pursing his lips, he made a valiant attempt to hold back a smile as he looked around the dining room. After a moment, he looked back at Jade and lifted his chin. "Go on, I have to hear the end of this."

"Did *Mr.* Barclay prove himself to be a capable assistant?" She rolled her eyes. "Not exactly. They took a few more trips down to Florida the following February. Then Sylvia took my original advice and dropped the study."

Spencer's sympathetic snort of disgust was almost as welcome as the touch of his hand on hers. "How convenient to be flying off to sunny Florida during Washington's coldest month."

Jade slipped her hand over his and smiled.

"Thank you."

"For what?" he asked.

"It feels so good to finally be able to talk about these less than pleasant times with someone I trust. No, don't look away like that," she said. "I mean it. Your taking this kind of interest tells me what kind of a person you are. It makes me feel...I don't know, calm inside, just knowing that you care enough to ask."

"I care, Jade," he said with such a soft and serious tone, it made her heart leap. "I care very, very much. Please promise me that you'll never doubt that."

The earnest look he gave her brought tears to her eyes. If she had to believe one thing, it was that his message was from his heart. She reached to stroke his chin as he leaned in to kiss her. Their kiss ended in a shared sigh.

"Spencer, I don't know what it is about you," she said, stroking his cheek, "but I find it so easy opening up to you. Even on the train into town, you had me talking."

Spencer looked away. "Hold that thought," he said as the waiter arrived with their salads. Spencer motioned for a grind of fresh pepper.

"I will," she whispered, as she gave Spencer's thigh a secret squeeze beneath the table.

By the time the waiter had refilled their water glasses, replaced the bread basket and assured them that the Chateaubriand would be out soon, Spencer had quietly worked his hand under her dress and up to the top of her thigh-high stocking. As he drew his open hand over her thighs, the pulsing pleasure his caress produced had her squirming. The second he touched the silky material between her legs, she knew countermeasures were in order. Reaching beneath his dinner napkin, she cupped her hand over his straining fly and felt the empty space inside her shiver.

As the waiter moved away, Spencer brushed his lips against her ear. "Do you have any idea what I'd like to do to you right now?"

"Yes. I'll stop if you will."

He closed his eyes and let out a sigh. "We'll pick this up later?"

"Deal."

Taking their hands away, they scooted several inches away from each other. While they waited for the crazy moment they'd created to settle down, Spencer stared at the bread basket and took slow, controlled breaths. She stared at her baby lettuce leaf salad, rubbed her temples and wondered if it was possible to have an orgasm by simply looking at a man. She doubted it. Her gaze slid to Spencer and she began to smile. Spencer Madison wasn't just any man. If it *were* possible to have an orgasm that way...

"Why are you looking at me like that?"

"I just had a strange thought," she said, picking up her salad fork.

"Strange is fine," he said before rolling his tongue along the inside of his cheek and looking away, "because in my present condition I can't guarantee how safe you'd be if you had a kinky one."

True. They did have to get through dinner in a public place. "Then I'll tell you my next thought which isn't that strange, really. Spencer, you'd be a terrific interviewer. You know, a professional interviewer.

Have you ever thought about that line of work? The reason I'm asking is that you make it so easy to talk."

Spence reached for the bottle of champagne then emptied it, topping off their glasses. He motioned to the waiter for another bottle; he was going to need it to get through this.

"Funny you should mention something connected with communication. Before I decided to take a crack at writing the great American novel, I was a roving communications technician for the State Department," he said, mixing an outright lie with his brother's legitimate career.

Jade's fork clattered against her plate. "You see how little I know about you?" she asked, playfully pinching his arm. "That sounds fascinating. Where have you worked?"

He shrugged as he tore off a piece of bread. "Barcelona. Bonn. Capetown. And anywhere in the Middle East you can name."

"Do you miss your old job?"

"My old job..." he said, placing the bread on his plate as he thought about his past career as a foreign journalist. "Certain aspects of it. But never fear, kiddo. I have enough socked away to feed my Smoochies habit until I turn in the manuscript."

"Ah, yes. The great American novel. You're so secretive about it. Every time I come near you when you're working, you almost slam your computer shut so I can't see what's on the screen."

"It's a work-in-progress and I've made it a point never to talk about it or show it to anyone, with the exception of my editor."

"Can't you give me a hint? Is it a murder mystery?

Intrigue? Political thriller? Come on," she said, "I've practically told you state secrets and you haven't given me a morsel of information on your book."

He made a zipping motion across his lips. "Sorry. I don't want to take a chance I'll jinx it. Anyway, I'm bored talking about me. Let's talk about you."

"Spencer, there's nothing left to talk about."

"Sure there is. Big changes have been happening in your life lately. When are you going to tell your family?"

"About us?"

He laughed then leaned to kiss her cheek. "I think they figured out that big change when we didn't come down to breakfast until almost eleven this morning."

She nibbled at the inside corner of her mouth. "They are being awfully grown-up about it…almost too understanding. They worry so much about my happiness, my future…."

"I know," he said, purposely avoiding talk about the future. He had enough guilt picking at his stomach. "You're fortunate to have them, but that's not the change I was referring to."

"You weren't?" she asked, looking slightly embarrassed.

He shook his head. "I was talking about you being fired."

"Oh, that." Looking down at her dinner napkin, she smoothed it with both hands.

"Yes, that. Jade, you did nothing to be ashamed of," he said, knowing that if she told her family, they might urge her to act on what she knew about Sylvia Bloomfield.

"I know, but I've put off telling them for so

long...." She pushed her salad away. "It's as if this lie I've been living has turned into an out-of-control monster. I'm just not sure how to do it now."

"You shouldn't worry about them. They've got to be the most understanding parents on the planet," he said, taking her hand in his again and kissing it. "And the sooner you get this off your chest, the sooner you can concentrate on what you have to do next."

"You mean, find a new job? I've been quietly working on that since shortly after we arrived."

"What about Sylvia Bloomfield and the way she's running her office?"

"Spencer," she said, pulling her hand from his. "I don't plan to do anything about that. She may be an adulteress, but unfortunately that won't necessarily get her kicked out of office. Anyway, I just want to forget the whole tacky episode."

His heart plummeted to the floor. *You can't forget about it, Jade, because if you do, there goes my chance at submitting a top-notch, brilliantly researched exposé that will get me out of the land of anonymous and back to legitimate journalism!*

Planting his elbows on the table's edge, he rubbed his face with both hands as he fought back the urge to growl in utter frustration. Now was not the time to lose it. He forced himself to shrug, even though he felt rightly concerned that his shoulders could snap with the tension gathered there.

"It doesn't seem right," he mumbled, his just-loud-enough words a calculated attempt to raise her concern.

"What doesn't?"

"When Representative Bloomfield gets caught polishing her desktop with her boy toy lover, you're the one who gets the boot. Shouldn't something be done? Shouldn't someone be told about this?''

"Who?''

He shrugged again. ''The congressional ethics committee?''

''And drag myself into that mess in front of the country? For what? So my family and friends can watch me humiliate myself on C-SPAN? No, thank you,'' she said. ''I have my pride.''

''Two words to think about, Jade,'' he said. ''Travel fraud.''

''Sylvia's too smart to get caught at that.'' She held up both hands. ''Oh, no. I have no intention of stirring up that killer beehive, especially when the queen has her stinger aimed at me. And besides, I'm finally starting to enjoy this vacation...all because of you. I just want to put the past behind me and enjoy the present.'' She pressed her fingers to his lips. ''Hush. Not another word.''

Spence leaned back in his chair at the Chocolate Chip Café as he watched Jade playing with Megan Sloan's five-year-old daughter. After dinner at the Hotel Maxwell he had decided to give Jade a few days before he brought up Sylvia Bloomfield's name again. What he hadn't figured on was the intensity of his ever-deepening feelings for Jade. The more time they spent together, the more he treasured and respected her. Maybe even loved her, but to save his soul from permanent damnation he couldn't allow himself to think about that right now.

He broke a hazelnut cookie in half then took a bite

of it as he watched Jade with the little girl. His thoughts began to stray and he found himself wondering what Jade would be like with her own child. He swallowed. All right, with *their* own child. There, he'd thought it outright and the devil hadn't appeared to claim him.

Anyway, thoughts on domestic bliss weren't so out of place since he and Jade had been together almost every minute since he'd come to her room that night. All of it had been perfect…in a temporary sort of way. He turned in his chair as he reminded himself that every sweet, hot moment they'd shared could end up as a sour spot in her memory once she found out about the exposé he was writing and how he'd pursued her to get it.

The operative word was *could,* he told himself.

She could just as easily forgive him and choose to hold on to the happy times they shared. He knew *he* always would because… He closed his eyes. *Go on, finish the statement, Spence. Be honest and admit it, if only to yourself.*

He was in love with her, with what she was and who she was. With her unique talents that he couldn't praise enough, with her neediness, which he adored, and with that love in her eyes that humbled him.

Leaning forward in his chair, he studied her in the big bay window beneath the arch of stenciled reindeer. Nestled in Jade's lap, a mesmerized Paige Sloan watched as the breathtaking redhead wove paper chains out of soda straw wrappers to drape around the five-year-old's neck.

Jade glanced up. "What are you smiling about?" she asked.

His reply was to continue smiling.

Jade motioned him closer.

"Paige's sitter is sick today and Megan told me her backup sitter is out of town for the holidays. Would you mind if we take Paige for the afternoon?"

Before he could reply, Paige piped in. "Mommy said Jade has real deer in her yard."

"Jade Macleod, where have you been hiding those deer?"

Spence's exaggerated look of surprise sent the little girl into a fit of giggles.

"In the woods near the river," Jade said, shifting the child so she could look up at her. "Would you like to see if we can find them this afternoon?"

"Yes, but I have to ask Mommy first. You stay here." Paige held up two small hands. "Don't go without me," she said, before scrambling off the cushioned window seat.

Spence watched a miniature Megan Sloan hurry around the bend of the counter to her mother.

"Do you mind us taking her?"

"Not at all. Megan mentioned the sitter situation when she asked me to bring in that box from the storeroom before," he said, kissing Jade's nose. "If you hadn't suggested taking Paige, I was about to."

An hour later they'd managed to send at least seven deer hightailing it to another part of the woods behind the Macleod house.

Paige groaned loudly as she tugged at Spence's pant leg. "I don't think they want to play with me."

"Hmm. Maybe yelling 'Bambi, do you want to make a snowman with us?' isn't such a good idea, Paige."

Jade leaned down close to Paige. "You see, deer are very shy. They're not at all like, well…puppies."

"Oh, I know all about puppies," Paige said excitedly.

"You do?" Spencer asked, winking at Jade as he took one of Paige's mittened hands and Jade took the other. "Do you have a puppy, Paige?"

"No," she said quietly, "but Santa said he'd see about bringing me one." She sighed dramatically. "I thought he meant for Christmas but I didn't get one."

"Their landlord won't allow it," Jade told him quietly.

"But Santa *said* he'd see about bringing me a puppy, and I don't think Santa can tell fibs to little kids." The little girl stopped and looked up at Spence. "Can he Mr. Mada-man?"

Jade laughed softly as Spence's life flashed before his eyes.

"Paige, I think you meant to say Mr. Madison, not Mr. Mada-man."

"Oops," the five-year-old said. "When I say your name like that, it sounds like you're a mad man."

Spence kept his eyes off Jade as he forced his heart out of his throat and back to his chest. "Tell you what, Paige. Why don't you just call me Spence?"

The little girl nodded but she wasn't smiling. Her chin began to quiver. "Okay, Spence." She pulled her hand from theirs and rubbed at her nose. "Spence?"

He placed his hands on his thighs and leaned down. "Yes, ma'am?"

"Do you think Santa ever lies to little kids?"

Before he could think of a good answer, Jade was

on her knees in front of the little girl. "No, darling, of course Spence doesn't think that. Do you, Paige?"

"I don't know," she said in a watery voice as one fat tear slipped from her eye and rolled down her cheek. "But I sure wanted that puppy. I was going to name him Beans." The first wracking sob shook her little body. "And he was gonna sleep by my bed," she said, before giving in to all-out, heart-wrenching sobs.

Jade took her into her embrace as Spence kneeled down beside them. "What do you do when they cry like this?" he asked, stroking the little girl's braids hanging out below her bright blue hat.

"You hold them," Jade said, as tears began glistening in her eyes. She gently leaned her cheek on Paige's head. "You hold them very close and try not to cry yourself."

Spence looked into her eyes. There was nothing else to say, and even if there were, he couldn't talk anyway. There was a lump the size of Alaska forming in his throat. He put his arms around the both of them and held on to the precious moment, knowing he'd seen a rare glimpse of Jade's future. The only trouble was not knowing if he'd be a part of it.

Nine

With the *Follett River Ledger* tucked beneath her arm, Jade took the stairs two at a time. Spencer had been working alone in his room all morning and now it was nearly lunchtime. She'd promised to leave him alone until then but Neal's "What Ever Happened To The Girl Most Likely To Succeed?" article had finally been printed and she couldn't wait another minute to see Spencer's reaction when he saw it.

After rounding the oak newel on the second-floor landing, she paused to look at the photo spread again. There was simply no hiding it; each photo was part of the proof that her feelings toward Spencer began back on that first afternoon.

Her face upturned, her gaze riveted on his as he spoke to the crowd gathered at the train station...

The steady stare the two had shared as if the brass

band hadn't been playing and attendant hoopla hadn't been happening…

His tender, knowing smile as she looked away in a new fit of panic…

Laughing softly, she knocked on his door. A second later she called his name then opened the door and stuck her head in.

The muffled sound of a running shower hummed in the background. She walked into his room and stared across at the bathroom door. Steamy images of her hips locked around his as he made passionate love to her against the pink-tiled walls of the shower stall had her taking a deep breath. That incredible scene had happened three times in the last week, each time more deeply pleasurable than the last. The idea of joining him was as tempting today as it had been before.

Her fingers closed over the edge of the door as she considered how she would explain her wet hair to everyone at lunch. She smiled. She'd think of something. Turning to close the hallway door behind her, her hand stopped in midair when she spotted the rectangle of silver-gray light glimmering in the mirror.

Spencer had left his computer on.

She nibbled at her bottom lip, shoved a nervous set of fingers through her hair and tiptoed across the room to the desk. Her silly reactions stemmed more from mischief than misgivings for what she was about to do. One little peek at his novel-in-progress, that was all she would take.

The shower continued humming, providing an amusing background sound for Spencer's perfectly pitched rendition of "My Girl," as she closed her hands over the top of the wheat-back desk chair and leaned in toward the computer screen.

A few lines into the document and she began to feel the weight of her smile slipping down her face.

It couldn't be....

It wasn't true.

It was impossible!

Spencer had taken the information she'd given him about her work with Sylvia Bloomfield and was working it into his novel. Her temples throbbed as she dragged out the chair, sat down and scrolled to the beginning.

As she read through the document, a far worse truth began sinking in like a lump of coal in vanilla pudding. Spencer wasn't writing a novel, he was writing about her life. At least, about the part involved with her job on Capitol Hill.

Blood drained from her face, leaving her light-headed and slightly confused. But only slightly. Spencer was a brilliant writer—clear, concise and brutally faithful to the facts.

A few more pages into the document and the truth came together like jagged bits of metal to a core magnet. She looked toward the sleigh bed, the eyelet-trimmed linens still rumpled from their energetic lovemaking last night, the chocolate-scented candle nearly gutted on the bedside table. Suddenly it was all there before her. Spencer had targeted her, stalked her, then used her to get inside information about Sylvia Bloomfield.

Why hadn't she seen this coming? That casual friendliness mixed, at least at first, with innocent flirting. Then his willingness to help her out at the train station and before she knew how it had happened, he was living under the same roof with her while beguiling her loved ones with his charm and seducing her with his "you can trust me" line.

She took a difficult breath then let it out with a surprisingly loud groan. Everything that had followed—every intimate, gut-wrenching, tender, heart-stealing minute—was all part of his carefully planned deception. Her sense of betrayal burned inside to simmering anger and then calculated revenge.

"Idiot," she whispered to herself as she turned back to the computer screen, her eyes stinging with tears she refused to shed. Spencer Madison had gotten more than his story and a free stay. He'd gotten her to think she was falling in love with him. But not for long, she thought, smacking a tear from her face as she slammed closed the computer.

Pushing back the chair, she reached for the electrical cord and ripped it from the socket. Grabbing the computer from the desk, she hurried to her room and slid it beneath her bed. And waited, her arms tightly crossed around her waist. Dumbstruck and shaking, her head jerked up when she heard the shower stop and its glass door open.

A few seconds later she could hear him in the next room, rummaging through the wardrobe. She walked back to the connecting door and quietly entered his room. While she waited to catch her breath, she made the mistake of watching him stepping into his jeans and pulling them up and over his tightly muscled behind. She'd enjoyed the sight dozens of times, loved hearing that masculine rip of his zipper, the quick snap of metal catching metal...and knew she'd never witness Spencer doing it again.

Leaning into the wardrobe, he riffled through the hanging clothes until he'd selected a soft blue, banded collared shirt. Tugging it from the hanger, he shoved an arm through a sleeve as he turned toward the desk...and froze.

"Looking for something?" Jade asked.

His gaze darted across the room to her then back to the empty space on the desk.

"Yeah," he said uneasily.

Good, she thought. At least he wasn't going to treat it like another joke. "Well, you're not going to find it."

He slid his other arm into his shirt and heaved a sigh.

"Guess it's time I had that talk I've been putting off."

"You lied to me."

She watched closely as he hesitated then nodded.

"Yes. I lied to you."

"Bastard," she bit off.

"Wait," he said, holding up both hands. "I know what you must be thinking—"

"You cannot imagine what I'm thinking. You don't want to *know* what I'm thinking."

"Just listen to me—"

"More lies?" She turned back to the door connecting her room to his. "I don't think so."

"What about your lies, Jade?"

"Mine?" she asked whipping around to face him.

"Yes, you've been lying to your family and your friends since the minute you arrived. You're still doing it by not telling them you were fired. When were you going to tell them, Jade?"

"I—it's none of your concern." She took a step toward him. "It was never any of your concern. Just a business thing with you. *Every*thing was, right, Spencer? Everything you did to me was all because of your work."

Spencer pressed his hands to his head, swearing under his breath as he struggled to remain in control.

"Everything we did, everything that happened between us on a personal level, was real." He pointed toward the bed, "There." He jerked his chin toward the bathroom door. "In there. And anywhere else we—"

"Stop it."

"No, I won't stop. All of that was real. Jade, don't you remember I asked you never to doubt my feelings for you?"

"Unfortunately I'm never going to forget any of what you said or did to me. Or what kind of a fool you made out of me." She held up her hand. "I want you to go."

"Jade, we can't leave things like this."

"Oh, I think we can. Besides, you're going to need plenty of time to start from scratch on that article you were writing because I've taken your computer and I'm not giving it back."

"Forget about that."

"As if you're going to."

"We have to talk."

"That's what I said the first morning after you…the first morning after we…"

"Say it. The first morning after we made love."

"You offered me lies and I bought them. A two-for-one sale, personal and professional."

She closed her eyes, straining to stop her lips from quivering and an uncooperative tear from running down her cheek. If one cut loose, there would be more to follow, enough to flood the place. No, dammit, she was going to save all of them for after he left.

Swallowing, she looked up at him. His shirt was still unbuttoned and hanging open, displaying that tautly muscled body, and that thick mat of chest hair that ended in a whorl around his navel. She couldn't lie to herself about what happened to her every time she looked at him. Even now, Lord forgive her, there was a shamefully hungry part of her that wanted nothing more than to hear him explain away the mess with one more whopper of a lie, then scoop her into his arms, stretch her out on the rumpled bed and make needy, greedy love to her until she couldn't think anymore. But she couldn't *not* think about the trust she'd given him.

"Jade," he said softly as he took a step toward her.

"No. The charade is over. Get out."

"What we have isn't a charade. What your ex-boss is doing is. She's pretending to stand up for family values when her personal life is anything but a model for family values. Jade, Sylvia's public image is a public-relations firm's dream. She tells the voters what they want to hear, then she goes on her arrogant, merry way doing just the opposite of what she's preaching.

"She and Lance are getting careless, Jade. It's only a matter of time before they're found out, and when that happens—listen to me—when that happens, the media will have a field day. And you're going to get caught in the fray, because although you don't work for her any longer, you haven't taken any stand against what she's doing. Because of that, your reputation is going down with hers.''

"Why do you pretend to care? I'm just your source. Someone you stalked, someone you set up. Why didn't you come to me and explain what you wanted?''

"Would you have told me?''

She looked away.

"I didn't think so, but now that it's out in the open between us, I can write this—''

"My God, you're still doing your reporter thing.''

"I'm a journalist.''

"A liar by any other name is still a liar. I'm not giving you any more information.''

"Are you saying you're going to protect Sylvia Bloomfield?''

"You bastard. You're looking for a quote, aren't you?''

"I'm giving you the opportunity to save your good name.''

"I don't need you for that. I can do it myself, thank you very much.'' She pulled herself up straight, squaring her shoulders and looking him directly in the eyes. "Why don't we call this even and have done with it? You used me for information, I used you for the sex.''

"No,'' he said softly. "You're not Sylvia Bloomfield. You didn't use me for the sex. What happened between us was much more precious than just sex, and that's what's tearing you apart right now. Isn't it, Jade?''

She backed against the door, grabbing wildly for

the knob. "Get...out!" she said, before turning away from him, pushing open the door then slamming it shut behind her.

He went to the door. "It's not over, Jade. Not by a long shot. You know I'm not holding back now. You're going to come to your senses about everything. And when you do, you'll come to me. We'll make it right."

"Spence, this piece on Sylvia Bloomfield is a definite go for the next issue of *Independence*. Why can't I convince you that you don't need the information from that ex-aide of hers? Don't get me wrong, her input is dynamite but the exposé works without it. Come on, I've known you since those days in Baghdad. What's this foot-dragging all about?"

Spence shifted his bottom in the chair, looked across the editor's desk and slowly pushed himself up onto his feet. He walked over to the wide window overlooking the Potomac.

"Sorry, Mack, but this article..." He shook his head uneasily as he turned to face his old friend. "It's about trust and how people break it for their own selfish reasons."

"I'm familiar with the article, Spence. I've been looking at it for a solid two months now. So why don't you tell me something I don't know?"

"I don't want it published unless it's the best I can do."

"And you feel without this information from the ex-aide that it's not any good? Spence," he said, coming around his desk toward the window, "would you mind taking one more fact into consideration here before you drop this in the trash? I am the editor. I decide if it's worthy. And it's worthy. Can't we come to some kind of a compromise here? This is your professional future we're talking about.''

And my personal one. Spence shoved his hands in the pockets of his khaki trousers and rattled his keys. "I can't, Mack." He sighed and looked out the window again. "I never thought I'd beg out of a writing job by saying this to an editor, but it's more than the piece itself. It's personal."

He felt Mack studying him for a long time. Spence drummed his fingers on the windowpane.

His friend started to smile as he reached out and thumped him hard on the shoulder. "You son of a bitch. Wait'll I tell Katie."

"Tell her what?" Spence asked, even though he already knew the answer.

"Cupid's arrow finally found a bull's-eye on your heart."

Spence snorted as a hint of a smile passed over his face. "It's not that simple."

"It never is. Look, I still want that exposé. It will bring you back in the public eye and sell a lot of magazines for me. So go home," he said, reaching for Spence's leather jacket and tossing it at him with a smile. "Think about your future, you besotted bastard."

"I'd rather not."

"Then go to her. Hash it over again. Convince her how important this is and then get your butt back where it belongs. Out of the Mad Man thing and in here with me at *Independence*."

"I'll think about it," Spence said without enthusiasm.

He headed for the door, deciding not to tell Mack that he would gladly crawl across the state of New Jersey on his hands and knees if he thought he had a chance of convincing Jade of anything. But he knew that Jade had to be the one to make the decision to come to him if they were going to have a chance at working anything out.

"Spence?"

He turned.

"She must be one hell of a woman."

He nodded. "One hell of a woman, Mack."

"You're crazy, Jade. You know that, don't you?" Rebecca Barnett asked as they walked along the sidewalk in downtown Follett River. "You let the stud muffin of the decade, next to Raleigh anyway, slip right through your fingers. And for what? A little tiff over his ambition versus yours."

"Reb, it wasn't about ambition. He lied to me," Jade said, stopping as Rebecca reached for the doorknob of her storefront travel office, New Horizon Tours. Her oval-shaped diamond engagement ring sparkled in the afternoon sunlight, bringing back another disturbing memory for Jade. Raleigh had proposed to Reb at the reunion dinner dance, the same night Spencer had kissed her. Stinging pain shot through her as the memories started back in detail. Desperately wanting to leave memories of that night behind, she quickly turned to Megan.

"If Spencer hadn't left his computer on, who knows when I would have found out his real purpose for being with me? Maybe I would have to read about it like everyone else will, in *Independence* magazine."

"Or maybe he was going to tell you, but you beat him to it," Megan said.

"Maybe's not good enough now."

"Look, all I know," Rebecca said, "is that you've been moping around town for two miserable months. Your eyes still get puffy from crying. You've lost weight. You didn't even press charges when Richard showed up whining about how guilty he felt over the money he, uh...*borrowed* from you." She leaned closer. "The money he lost in Atlantic City."

Jade shrugged. "I was just grateful to have my car back."

Rebecca looked at Megan. "See what I mean? She's still not getting it."

Jade gestured with both hands. "Not getting what?" she asked, her frustration heightening her voice.

"Jade, the closest you've come to smiling is when the Mad Man columnist started back with new material last month. So don't try telling us that you're better off without Spencer Madison, because you're not." Rebecca pushed open the door to New Horizon Tours. "Words of wisdom, girlfriend. Stubbornness sucks. You can't cuddle up to it on a cold night."

"She's right," Megan said.

Jade frowned at both of them. "What is this? I thought we decided to spend your lunch breaks shopping for Reb's wedding dress, but you're both sounding as if this is one of those interventions. You know, like I have a substance-abuse problem."

Rebecca leaned around Jade to Megan. "I believe it's your turn, Meggie. I have to get back to work." She kissed Jade on the cheek. "Listen to Meggie. She's a lot more patient about this love thing than I am."

As Rebecca went into her travel agency and closed the door, Jade walked on toward the Chocolate Chip Café with Megan. "I can see your lips itching. Say it."

"Did you ever think about how proud rhymes with Macleod?"

"Oh, boy, that's some lead-in. Come on. Let me have your take on my life. Then I'll tell you why you and Reb don't know what you're talking about. Again."

"When you told your family that you weren't working for Sylvia Bloomfield any longer, what did they say?"

"Well, they surprised me," she said, slowing her steps as she looked across the street to the town square. "They said it was probably time for a change in my life and that they were sure I could get another job anytime I wanted one."

"Uh-huh. And what did your friends say when you told them?"

Jade shrugged. "Nothing much. The news didn't appear to bother anyone. Except me."

"But you had anticipated some pretty unpleasant moments over telling anyone that news. You even put off telling anyone about breaking up with Richard. You probably were thinking that you were going to die of embarrassment. Right?"

Jade smiled. "I did. I really did think that." She

stopped dead in her tracks. "Megan Sloan, what are you getting at?"

"Your pride. You had a hard time telling us about losing your job and breaking up with Richard, but you finally dealt with both issues and survived." Megan took her hand. "Jade, I know a little bit about pride and how it can destroy a person's cherished dreams. But I don't think pride is about how other people think of you. It's about how you think of yourself once you've acted on your beliefs. Beliefs that are rooted in integrity, in what you know is right."

At that moment, one of Megan's waitresses knocked on the window from inside the Chocolate Chip Café. Megan held up one finger to let the girl know she'd be right in, then turned back to Jade.

"Was Spence really all that bad? Can't you find it in your heart to forgive him for overzealous ambition?"

"Meggie, I don't know," she whispered, twisting the fringe on her neck scarf. "I just don't know. Maybe all that time we were, well…"

"It's okay. You can say it," the pretty blonde said with a smile. "I might be a widow but I can still remember sex."

"That's just it. When I allow myself to remember those times with him, I have to wonder if it stemmed from his guilt over deceiving me. Maybe he realized how attracted to him I was and…"

"Maybe it's time to blow off some of that pride and go down to Washington for some explanations."

"Just like that?" she asked, snapping her fingers. When she thought about seeing him again, a warm feeling curled through her, followed by a shiver of paralyzing fear. "Just take a chance and maybe fall flat on my face."

"Or into his arms?" Meggie asked, before she went inside the Chocolate Chip Café.

Jade stood alone, staring up Main Street for several seconds as she pondered Rebecca and Megan's advice. Stubbornness. Pride. Integrity. What did it all matter when she hadn't heard from him in two weeks? She shook her head, trying not to think about seeing him again. Sooner or later the pain would fade. Wouldn't it? And she would get on with her life. Right?

Ten minutes later she'd driven inside the Macleods' three car garage, got out and headed straight for the cabinet in the kitchen where she kept her downstairs stash of Smoochies. She pulled open the oak door, reached for the bag and groaned.

"Mother!"

"Yes, dear," Mrs. Macleod said as she entered the kitchen. "What did you want?"

"I want you to stop leaving these where I have to look at them," she said, waving one of the photos her mother had taken of Spencer and her the night of the reunion dinner-dance.

"Oh, did I leave one of them there?" Mrs. Macleod asked a little too innocently. "I can't imagine what was on my mind." She took the photo from Jade. "What a handsome man. Even your father said so. And Neal says he's a great athlete, too. It's too bad he had to leave like that."

Jade gave a labored sigh. "Forget him, Mother. I intend to, myself, as soon as you and everyone else allow me to. He's not coming back. He's not going to call.''

She took the photo from her mother and slapped it facedown onto the counter. Grabbing the bag of Smoochies out of the cupboard, Jade headed for the stairs as the phone began to ring. She looked back at her mother.

''Answer it, dear. It might be…for you.''

Jade lifted the receiver from the wall unit and held it to her ear, willing herself to picture the person on the other end. Her mind's eye remained blank.

''Hello? Macleod residence.''

''Jade? Is that you?''

Her eyes opened wide in surprise. ''Yes, Sylvia. It is.''

''Wonderful,'' she said in that simpering voice reserved for begging favors. ''I'm so glad I caught you. Jade, let me get right to the point. I've been reconsidering my reaction to that unfortunate…well, let's say incident you stumbled upon. I want you to know that I'm taking all the blame for my little indiscretion. You were a perfectly innocent party.''

Jade frowned at the suspicious tone of Sylvia's call. She'd worked for the politician long enough to know when the woman was concerned, and Sylvia was concerned big-time.

''That's nice to hear.'' *Nice to hear, certainly true, but not necessarily sincere,* she thought, scratching her head. ''Does this mean I can expect a decent letter of recommendation soon?''

''I was hoping you would consider coming back to work for me. Things have been so difficult since you left. Corinne doesn't know what she's doing and Lance, well…'' She sighed.

Jade rolled her eyes. ''Yes, how is Lance?''

The woman giggled nervously. ''Better than ever.''

''I meant, behind a desk, Sylvia. Sitting down in front of his computer.''

''He's doing much better,'' Sylvia said in a more businesslike tone. ''Listen,'' she said, her voice a bit more desperate now, ''perhaps you can forget what you saw that night.''

''I have a hard time forgetting things.''

''Oh. I see. Perhaps if I could offer a way to help you forget, we could put all this unpleasantness behind us.''

''What is it you're trying to say?'' Jade asked, thoroughly confused and surprisingly interested in what Sylvia was getting at.

''I think I could come up with a very nice fact-finding mission for you. Say, a trip to Maui for a week. Perhaps two.''

''Maui? What's your interest in Maui?''

Sylvia laughed. ''I can't think of a thing, dear. But if you'll come back to the office, I'm sure we can come up with something.''

Cold prickles started over her scalp as everything Spencer had suggested about Sylvia slammed back into her consciousness. He was right. And she had been ignoring the truth for too long. But she couldn't discount this kind of evidence.

''We'll have your office redone any way you want, Jade. Perhaps you'd like to suggest a few other changes I haven't thought of. I really need you back here.''

Jade closed her eyes as a sensation of nausea rippled through her chest. *Spencer, you were right, she is a saccharine-coated spider.*

"Maui, Jade. Just think of all that tropical beauty. What do you say?"

"The last time I saw Lance, his tan line was fading. Why don't you send him?" Jade said, before hanging up the phone.

She looked at her mother who was leaning against the kitchen counter a few feet away. The woman was holding the photo again, tapping it lightly against her palm and smiling.

"What are you thinking, Mother?"

"How lovely you'd look in ivory."

Jade shook her finger at her mother. "Don't go planning a wedding."

"I wouldn't dream of it," she said, walking to her daughter and slipping her arm through Jade's. "Would you like me to help you pack?"

Ten

Spence stared out of the loft window of his Georgetown house overlooking the old canal. Through the
March rain beading on the windowpane he caught the
curious sight of green buds, straining toward a new
life cycle, mixing with the reflected red-gold light
from his fireplace. Except for this first sighting of the
fragile green growth, it had been the dreariest spring
on record—Spencer's record anyway. He started to
think about Jade, then shook his head to force his
thoughts away from the treasured images. No, he
wasn't going there. Not for a fourth time today.

Frowning, he leaned his head back to stare at the
ceiling. Mack's renewed griping hadn't been helping
his mood, either. Yesterday the editor had faxed him
an ultimatum. The editor of *Independence* magazine
needed his decision by the end of the week. Would

Spence say yes to publishing his piece on Sylvia Bloomfield or was he trashing the project? The project that changed his life.

Once again his thoughts boomeranged to Jade and the last words he'd spoken to her. *"It's not over, Jade. Not by a long shot. You know I'm not holding back now. You're going to come to your senses about everything. And when you do, you'll come to me. We'll make it right."*

He pulled in a lungful of air then blew it out of his puffed cheeks. Had he been too rough on her with those words? Had he asked too much? Lowering his head, he pressed his palm to the windowpane. Had she heard any of it through that closed door?

All he knew for certain was that his life was dead in the water. He had two choices: tread water or move on. But he couldn't move on without seeing her again. Seeing her again… He closed his eyes. He wasn't too proud to go to her, just too scared that she would turn him away. Forever.

Thunking his forehead against the window, he caught a glimpse of movement on the path beside the canal. This treading business was getting old, he thought as a pair of long, shapely legs beneath a short, olive green raincoat, came into view.

She moved slowly, almost hesitantly, off the path and toward his door.

The bright yellow umbrella she was using to screen herself from the blowing rain covered her face and upper body. Still… Hairs tickled then stood up on the back of his neck. His mouth went dry. He didn't have to see her face. He knew. Every fiber in his body shouted her name.

"Jade."

He felt his body jerk as hope shot through him with the force of champagne spurting from its bottle.

"Jade," he said again, louder this time. He was across the loft, down the narrow steps and into the foyer before her finger was off the doorbell.

Shoving his hands through his hair, he told himself he wasn't hallucinating. He slowly smoothed the front of his Georgetown University sweatshirt and stared at the doorknob. His heart pounded. His hands were moist. He *wasn't* wrong. He couldn't be. Those were Jade's legs, not those of a stranger collecting for the disease of the week.

She knocked this time.

Pulling open the door, he stared at the woman on the other side of it. Her yellow umbrella reminded him of sunshine bursting around her head, a bright nimbus that couldn't compare with this redhead's radiant beauty. Raindrops clung to her lashes and cheekbones, sparkling like a veil of crushed diamonds.

"Jade," he said, the sound of her name floating through his mind like music, lifting his spirits and answering his prayers.

"Hello, Spencer. I brought you your computer," she said, glancing down at the object, wrapped in a plastic grocery bag, in her arms.

Computer? Who gave a flying fudge brownie about his computer? Jade had come back to him.

"Come in," he said, before stepping out into the

blowing rain to help her close her umbrella. The awkward move combined with the wet and whipping wind left his back soaked, her bangs dripping and him acutely aware of how much he'd missed being this close to her.

"Your hands are like ice," he said, guiding her inside to the small entry hall. Setting her umbrella in the corner, he offered to take the computer but she shook her head. Instead, she shifted it from one arm to the other while he helped her out of her raincoat. The growing tension flowing through him began prickling again as he hung up the damp coat. Why wouldn't she look at him?

He coughed and turned around to her. "When did you get back in town?"

"This morning," she said, looking around the small, tiled area.

He nodded as an awkward silence fell between them again. He kept on nodding until realizing he must look like one of those toy dogs with a bobbing head in the rear window of a car. Reaching for the back of his neck, he scrubbed at it with his knuckles, too stupefied by her presence to think of something else to say.

When her gaze finally landed back on him, she clutched the computer to her chest, holding it as if it were a shield between them.

"Are you busy? Did I come at the wrong time?" Alarm burned bright in her eyes as she began grazing her lip with her teeth. "I—I'm sorry. You have someone here—"

"No," he said, holding the door closed when she

reached for the knob. "I don't have anyone here." She appeared to breathe a little easier then.

"Do you think we could talk?"

"Yeah." He dipped his head once. "Sure."

He motioned toward his living room then backed against the front door to allow her plenty of room to pass in front of him. If he touched her again, he might drag her into his arms and not let her go for several hours.

He tried centering his thoughts on some calm spot inside his head. There was no calm spot. There wasn't going to be one for quite a while. Pushing off the door, he headed into the living room, hoping a miracle would keep him from saying or doing something that would destroy this second chance with her.

She was standing in front of the fireplace, still holding the computer and shivering. From the cold? From nerves? Or was he experiencing one of those hysterical vision episodes he'd read about somewhere?

"Can I get you something to drink?"

"Sherry?"

Sherry. She wanted sherry. "I'll be right back," he said, heading for the door to the kitchen. Halfway across the black and white tiles, he turned back to the door. "Don't go anywhere."

She looked up at him for a second. "I'm not."

Sherry. Where the hell had he put that bottle of it? Rummaging through the cabinet, he was already planning a dash on foot to the nearest liquor store when he pulled the bottle out from behind the Scotch.

A minute later he paused in the doorway, the bottle of sherry in one hand and the fingers of his other laced around the stems of two glasses. She was sitting on his leather hassock, the big round one made of camel leather that he'd picked up in North Africa over a decade ago. "Fit for your princess," the old Bedouin had told him in impeccable English.

"Fresh bottle," he said, holding up the bottle as he crossed the room. He set the glasses on the sofa table, peeled back the seal and began working out the cork. "Well, I've had it for five years, but I've never opened it. I guess we can call that fresh."

When she smiled, he felt higher than if he'd polished off a couple of six-packs with some of his old traveling buddies.

"How's the family?" he asked, pouring both of them a glass.

"Fine," she said, turning her attention to the fireplace. "Everyone in Follett River is," she said, effectively killing his next six, chitchat, fill-in-the-silent-space questions!

Bringing the glasses to where she sat, Spence handed her one then took a seat on the sofa. Their knees were inches apart as they sipped the rich, amber red liquid.

"A little warmer now?" he asked, watching the way her moist lips glistened in the firelight.

"Yes." She took another sip then set the glass aside.

He did the same, then cleared his throat, and leaned forward to rest his forearms on his knees.

"Why did you come, Jade?"

She pulled off the plastic bag, dropped it to the rug and placed the computer in his hands. "I want you to publish your exposé," she said, her voice light but strong.

He turned his head and squinted as if he hadn't heard her right.

"Why now?"

She reached into her pocket and brought out a computer disk. "Remember I told you that Sylvia had taken Project Suntan away from me and given it to Lance Barclay?"

"Yeah. That was exactly the kind of stuff I'd been looking for for my article."

"Well, now you have proof of your suspicions," she said, placing the disk on top of the computer.

He stared at her and then at the disk. "What are you saying? What do I have?"

She stood up and began to walk around his living room. "Among other things, proof that Lance Barclay is a bad speller." She turned back to face him. "And that he has a penchant for making lists."

"Lists of what?"

"The number of times he and Sylvia rented a helicopter to drop them at a private island in the Caribbean called Honeymoon Key. The number of times he had roses, specifically hot pink roses, delivered to her at their suite. There's more of the same on there," she said, pointing to the disk. "Like the dates and fees for their personal massage sessions with the resort's professionals. Lance isn't as stupid as we thought he was. He came up with a clever way to have all of it charged off to official purchases."

"Hold on," Spence said, as he set the computer on

the rug and picked up the disk. "How did you get your hands on this?"

"Remember that phone call you told me about when we were at Megan's café Christmas Eve morning?"

"I remember that after you returned the call, you were devastated. I thought you were going to cry...." He met her eyes and wondered if she'd cried about him over the last two months.

Twisting her pinkie ring, she looked away.

"I'm sorry I interrupted. Please, go on."

"Corinne sent me the rest of the things I'd left behind in my office. She must have accidentally run across this disk, and since Lance hadn't taken the time to relabel it, Corinne must have seen my name on it and threw it in with my other things. Last night, when I was packing to come down here, I decided to have a look at it."

He stood up and set the disk aside. "So you'd already decided to come back to Washington before you had a look at what was on the disk?"

She nodded. His heart hammered against his rib cage.

"Because...?"

"Sylvia Bloomfield called me yesterday. She asked me to come back to work for her."

"You didn't say yes. Did you?" he asked, wondering if he'd been time-warped to a parallel world. He shook his head. "No, of course you didn't. What am I thinking? You wouldn't be giving me this information if you were going back to your job."

"Spencer," Jade said, walking to the wingback

chair between them. She pressed her hands to the top of it and leaned toward him. "She's everything you thought she was and worse. She offered to send me to Maui for two weeks on official travel. When I asked for what reason, she laughed and told me we'd come up with something. That's why I decided to bring your computer back so that you could write the piece from your original files. The disk from Lance was just the cherry on the sundae."

Jade watched him for several seconds, swearing to herself that she could almost see the wheels turning behind those blue eyes of his. She knew what he was thinking. And it wasn't how to thank her. Or ask that she forgive him. Or even understand what he'd done. He was already pulling his facts together to finish his exposé.

"Sylvia deserves this piece you're going to write," she said, making busywork of checking her watch. If she started crying now, he'd have to have her carted off in an ambulance. "I, uh, have a job interview soon. I don't want to be late."

She started past him.

"And the Mad Man has one last column to write."

A raindrop shook loose from her bangs and dropped onto her forehead as she stopped suddenly and turned around. "What?"

"Your favorite columnist. Your shot of Tabasco in the morning. He's changing jobs."

She pointed to him, then clamped her hand over her mouth. A second later she pointed to him again. "You? You're the Mad Man?" she asked, too stunned to close her mouth.

He nodded.

"That's why they kept reprinting your old columns, because you were in Follett River with me."

"Right."

"And you're writing your last column?"

He nodded. "Thanks to you."

"I got you fired?"

"I quit."

"I'm so confused."

"I'm not. Not anymore." He pointed to the sofa. "You want to sit down or will I make you late for your job interview?"

She rubbed her temples. "I can be late," she said, taking a seat on the sofa. She watched him pace in front of the fireplace; he was as tense as she was again and that was somehow comforting to her. Hopeful. Even promising.

And then he stopped and, facing her, sat on the hassock at her feet.

"First of all," he said, lacing his fingers together and letting them dangle between his sprawled knees, "I should have been straight with you from the beginning. But I kept telling myself you might not understand, and then I'd never be able to write the damn article and get it published under my real name."

She felt her eyes widening to comedic proportions. "Your real name?"

"William Spencer Madison. About eight years ago I started going by Bill Madison."

She pulled back a few inches. "I remember Bill Madison. He was a foreign journalist who had that Sunday-night program from different places around the world." She hesitated then clamped her hand over her mouth. "No."

"Yes. I thought you almost had me that first night when I found you in the bedroom opening my wallet." Shaking his head, he smiled. "Anyway, I wore glasses back in my Bill Madison days because I thought it made me look more mature. And I had a mustache. Don't ask why. It just seemed like a good idea at the time."

Jade brought her hand away from her mouth then touched his hair. "And this was shorter and you parted it here…. What happened to Bill Madison?"

"Minor celebrity status happened. But not minor enough. One of the papers started calling me Mad About Him Madison. Somebody in Nevada started an Internet web page on me."

"A fan club."

He nodded. "Complete with investment opportunities and marriage proposals. Someone in Reno even had a cocktail named after me. Then *People* magazine did a piece on me. I naively believed it would be about my work as a journalist but it was a fluff piece meant for a laugh. After that hit the newsstands I couldn't get a serious interview with anyone but has-been movie stars living in the south of France and the owner of a stud farm outside Helsinki. The worst happened when I was offered a spot as a cohost of a magazine show. You have to remember that my idea of cosmetic enhancement was mud dripping from my boots. At the time I thought anchoring the news would be the kiss of death for me, but doing celebrity gossip… Suicide." He shook his head at the obviously depressing memory.

"And that's when you came back to Washington, became Spencer Madison and started the Mad Man column."

"Right. The editor at the *Washington Herald* is a friend of mine. When he got fed up with listening to me complain about the unfair hand I'd been dealt, he suggested I do a column. The anonymous part was my idea. I wasn't taking any chances at that point. That was five years ago."

"And what made you decide to write the exposé on Sylvia?"

"The Mad Man had to remain anonymous, and because of that I was severely limited as to what I could tackle. Sure, I stirred things up around town but that's all I could do. I needed a change and I figured enough time had passed. I started talking to an old friend over at *Independence*. We'd both heard rumors about Bloomfield. Mack's been desperate for a crackerjack piece on her for quite some time."

She looked away. "And that's when you started following me?"

"Jade, you have to understand, I never meant for things to go as far as they did."

"I understand," she said, checking her watch as she stood up. She had to get out of there. Get away from him. *"I never meant for things to go as far as they did."* She looked away from him as he stood with her. At least he had the decency to tell her he regretted using her.

"Jade, it was a way to come back into legitimate

print journalism. But once I got close to you, things started getting out of hand. I'm so sorry I hurt you. That I waited so long to explain. Then you got so angry and—"

"It's okay. It's over now," she said, holding up her hands as she tried to step around him.

"Hold on," he said.

He was only touching her hand, but he might as well have been holding her heart. "Spencer, please. I have to go." *I have to go before I break into a million pieces all over this rug.*

"Before you go tearing out of here, I want you to see something. Come on," he urged, tugging her toward the foyer. "It'll only take a minute."

She never could think straight when his hands were on her. Why did she think she could now? "Just for a minute," she murmured as he began leading her up the stairs to the loft.

"Over here," he said, walking her by his bed. She tried not to stare, but forest green comforters and sugar white sheets would never look the same to her again. He stopped walking when he got to a huge oak desk by the window.

"You got yourself another computer. That's nice." He let go of her hand and brain function began returning. She looked around for another way downstairs.

He opened a deep drawer in the side of the desk, reached in and took out a blue folder. "Take a look," he said, handing it over.

She did. After a moment she looked up. "It's the exposé. You've already written it."

He nodded. "I copied the file before you took my computer. Now have a look at this," he said, brushing away Smoochie wrappers from a paper sitting on his desk, then holding it up for her to see.

She scanned it, then took it from him to read it more carefully. Her lips parted as she looked up at him.

"That's right. That's another fax from *Independence* begging me for permission to print the exposé, even without your inputs. Jade, I could have had this published two months ago, but I didn't. I couldn't."

"Why not?" she whispered, meeting his eyes with an unblinking look from her own.

He slid his hands over her arms and pulled her a little closer. "Because I couldn't do that to you. I couldn't break your trust again and live with myself."

"You were ready to give up this opportunity because of me?" she asked, tears stinging her eyes. She let them fall this time.

"Yes." Cupping her face in his palms, he thumbed away her tears. "Jade, say you'll forgive me for all the trouble I've caused you. I swear, I'll never hold anything back from you again."

Reaching up she ran her fingertips over his beard stubble, reveling in the familiar feel of it.

"If you'll forgive me for being so stubborn. Spencer, I missed you so much—" she began, but her sentence ended as his lips captured hers. For a long while they kissed, taking every pleasure possible from the act. And then he reached for the buttons on her sweater.

"You're going to be late for your job interview," he said against her lips. "Very, very late."

She laughed softly against his cheek. "That's okay. I'm thinking of taking a break from my career for a while."

"My, my," he teased, "what will you do with all that time?"

She shrugged as he peeled back her sweater. "Eat a lot of Smoochies, take tango lessons…make love."

"And marry me?"

"Yes," she whispered. "Marry you."

After a long while his gaze dropped from hers to her breasts. His mouth opened.

"Jade Macleod," he whispered, running his fingers over the spaghetti straps of the red, miniplaid bra. "I wondered if you'd gotten this."

"It arrived in the mail about a week after you left. Since you had it addressed to me, I opened it," she said as he stared at the demicup, flannel lingerie. Stepping back, she drew her fingers over the creamy swells of her breasts. "What do you think?"

Smiling, he reached behind her back to unhook it. "I think a girl who wears flannel needs it removed by the right man. Me." He tossed the bra over the top of his chair, then scooped her up in his arms and headed for his bed.

"Did I ever tell you how much I love you?" he asked, setting her on her feet before they raced to remove the rest of their clothing.

"No," she said, laughing as they dropped the last articles of clothing to the floor. "Did I ever tell you?"

"No." Spence glanced toward the papers on his

desk then looked back at her. "Words." He shook his head. "They have a habit of getting in the way of it sometimes." He took her onto the bed and pressed her back against the pillows. "Maybe we'd better just show each other instead."

And they did.

*   *   *   *   *

This summer, the legend
continues in Jacobsville

Diana Palmer

A LONG, TALL TEXAN SUMMER

Three **BRAND-NEW** short stories

This summer, Silhouette brings readers a special
collection for Diana Palmer's LONG, TALL TEXANS
fans. Diana has rounded up three **BRAND-NEW**
stories of love Texas-style, all set in Jacobsville,
Texas. Featuring the men you've grown to love from
this wonderful town, this collection is a must-have
for all fans!

*They grow 'em tall in the saddle in Texas—and
they've got love and marriage on their minds!*

Don't miss this collection of original Long, Tall Texans
stories...available in June at your favorite retail outlet.

Take 4 bestselling love stories FREE

Plus get a FREE surprise gift!

Special Limited-time Offer

Mail to Silhouette Reader Service™

3010 Walden Avenue
P.O. Box 1867
Buffalo, N.Y. 14240-1867

YES! Please send me 4 free Silhouette Desire® novels and my free surprise gift. Then send me 6 brand-new novels every month, which I will receive months before they appear in bookstores. Bill me at the low price of $2.90 each plus 25¢ delivery and applicable sales tax, if any.* That's the complete price and a savings of over 10% off the cover prices—quite a bargain! I understand that accepting the books and gift places me under no obligation ever to buy any books. I can always return a shipment and cancel at any time. Even if I never buy another book from Silhouette, the 4 free books and the surprise gift are mine to keep forever.

225 BPA A3UU

Name	(PLEASE PRINT)
Address	Apt. No.
City	State	Zip

This offer is limited to one order per household and not valid to present Silhouette Desire® subscribers. *Terms and prices are subject to change without notice.
Sales tax applicable in N.Y.

UDES-696   ©1990 Harlequin Enterprises Limited

As seen on TV!
Free Gift Offer

With a Free Gift proof-of-purchase from any Silhouette® book,
you can receive a beautiful cubic zirconia pendant.

This gorgeous marquise-shaped stone is a genuine cubic
zirconia—accented by an 18" gold tone necklace.

(Approximate retail value $19.95)

Send for yours today…
compliments of ▼ *Silhouette*®

To receive your free gift, a cubic zirconia pendant, send us one original proof-of-
purchase, photocopies not accepted, from the back of any Silhouette Romance™,
Silhouette Desire®, Silhouette Special Edition®, Silhouette Intimate Moments®
or Silhouette Yours Truly™ title available in February, March and April at your favorite
retail outlet, together with the Free Gift Certificate, plus a check or money order for
$1.65 U.S./$2.15 CAN. (do not send cash) to cover postage and handling, payable
to Silhouette Free Gift Offer. We will send you the specified gift. Allow 6 to 8 weeks for
delivery. Offer good until April 30, 1997 or while quantities last. Offer valid in the
U.S. and Canada only.

Free Gift Certificate

Name: _____

Address: _____

City: _____ State/Province: _____ Zip/Postal Code: _____

Mail this certificate, one proof-of-purchase and a check or money order for postage
and handling to: SILHOUETTE FREE GIFT OFFER 1997. In the U.S.: 3010 Walden
Avenue, P.O. Box 9077, Buffalo NY 14269-9077. In Canada: P.O. Box 613, Fort Erie,
Ontario L2Z 5X3.

FREE GIFT OFFER   084-KFD
ONE PROOF-OF-PURCHASE
To collect your fabulous FREE GIFT, a cubic zirconia pendant, you must include this
original proof-of-purchase for each gift with the properly completed Free Gift Certificate.

084-KFD

And the Winner Is...
You!

...when you pick up these great titles
from our new promotion at your
favorite retail outlet this June!

Diana Palmer
The Case of the Mesmerizing Boss

Betty Neels
The Convenient Wife

Annette Broadrick
Irresistible

Emma Darcy
A Wedding to Remember

Rachel Lee
Lost Warriors

Marie Ferrarella
Father Goose

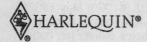